MISCONSTRUED

ERIC C.
EVANS

WORLDWIDE®

TORONTO • NEW YORK • LONDON
AMSTERDAM • PARIS • SYDNEY • HAMBURG
STOCKHOLM • ATHENS • TOKYO • MILAN
MADRID • WARSAW • BUDAPEST • AUCKLAND

For
Charles and Zanne Evans

The supreme happiness of life
is the conviction that we are loved.
—Victor Hugo

MISCONSTRUED

A Worldwide Mystery/February 2003

First published by Thomas Bouregy & Company, Inc.

ISBN 0-373-26448-8

Printed in U.S.A.

Acknowledgments

I would like to express a heartfelt thank you for the significant contribution to my work made by:

Kerry Casaday, a masterful proofreader and editor;

Jason Miller who put the Doctor in Spin Doctor;

Sabra Elliot Larkin, my agent, for her insightful criticism and expert advice;

Erin Cartwright and Ellen Mickelsen, respectively my editor and publisher at Avalon Books, for their continued faith in my work.

And as always, an especial thanks to my wife Debora for...everything.

Acknowledgments

[illegible]

[illegible]

[illegible]

[illegible]

[illegible]

[illegible]

ONE

"STOP THESE PEOPLE or you're fired, McKall," the Governor said, creating one of the moments of tension he seemed to thrive on. He liked being the only person in the room who was relaxed and comfortable.

Soon enough, though, he broke the tension with his trademark smile, letting me know he was just joking—well, mostly joking anyway.

Through years of refinement, Governor Beckstead has developed an over-the-top style purposely calibrated to keep his audience on edge. When I first began working for him this type of behavior had been unnerving, but I had by now grown used to it.

"I'm going to enjoy killing this nuclear waste dump proposal," he said, propping his feet up on his heavily scarred desk. "Can't go wrong. Everybody hates 'em. Republicans. Democrats. Everybody."

"That's true," I said, "but if this is really going to be the top priority of your administration, we can't just talk about it, we have to actually *do* something. People will expect it. And its going to be a little more difficult than we think." By "we" I meant "you, Governor."

"We have no jurisdiction on the reservation, so whatever we do will require some creativity. Holding press conferences and twisting a few arms in the legislature will have zero effect on what the tribe decides to do. As long as the Consortium has a deal with the Pishutes and they keep their project out there on the reservation, we have very little direct say about what happens. It's pretty much between the Pishutes and the Feds."

"Come on McKall, you gotta think bigger than that. This is political on every level and in politics, there is always another way," he said, doffing his eyebrows as if he had already worked out some grand strategy.

I had worked for Governor Beckstead long enough to know that he had now stopped paying any real attention to what I was saying on this subject. He had made up his mind that this proposal could indeed be killed. Finding a way to actually do it was just a minor detail.

"You're right of course," I said, "but our next step—before we call a press conference and pronounce the project DOA—is to figure exactly how we are going to kill it. Until we can answer that question, we are all better served if we express grave concern over the proposal and keep the rhetoric to a minimum."

Just as the Governor was about to launch into one of his finger-pointing lectures, my secretary, Nina, stuck her head into the office. "Jack Longnight is here. He's waiting in the lobby," she said.

Jack Longnight was the chief of the Pishute Indian Tribe and as far as we could determine, the main instigator of a deal to bring a nuclear waste dump to the Pishute Indian reservation in the west desert of Utah. Today was to be our first meeting with him since the project was announced.

"Right on time," I said, looking at my watch and wishing he had been a few minutes late so that the Governor and I could have more time to prepare for the meeting. But he wasn't late and I could not leave him waiting in the lobby.

"Bring him on in. Jack's a good guy, he'll work with us," the Governor said, ever confident in his ability to shoot from the hip.

"Governor, this is an important meeting. Swaying Jack is our best chance of stopping this thing," I said, making one more half-hearted attempt.

"Sam, I can handle this meeting. Just bring him in," he said without even a hint of humor in his voice.

I could sense that not only was he through listening, he was now through talking, so without another word I reluctantly went to escort Jack in for the meeting. The governor left his private office for the ceremonial office where the meeting with Jack was to be held.

SAVVY IS NOT a word I would use to describe LaGrand Beckstead. However, brains can be overrated as a tool for creating political longevity. LaGrand Beckstead had something I respected much more than political savvy; he had a unique ability to bend people to his will by the shear force of his personality. That is not to say that he is beloved. He isn't. Nor do people live in fear and loathing of him. But throughout his entire political career he has possessed an indefinable quality which compels people, often against logic and reason, to do what he wants of them.

Those skills had served Beckstead well as he methodically made his way up the political food chain, feeding on the less fit. Having started nearly twenty years ago as city councilman, he had managed to survive his way to somewhere near the top. But now, in true Darwinian fashion, he had climbed far enough up the food chain that his would-be prey was not so easily manipulated by his political wiles. And Beckstead was having trouble adjusting to the heightened level of competition, which had made his transition into the Governor's office quite rocky.

The biggest problem pointed to by his detractors was a childlike inability to handle situations where he could not control the outcome by simply willing it to be so. His behavior at those times is what earned Beckstead the nickname Baby Grand. And much to the Governor's chagrin the nickname, once applied, had stuck. Even the governor's most ardent supporters were forced to admit—off the record of course—that the moniker was well deserved.

As is often the case in politics, steadily dropping

poll numbers and an increasingly hostile press had caused a major shake-up in his staff. A longtime Beckstead friend and political advisor was bounced out as chief of staff and I was brought in to steady the ship.

That was nine months ago, and to this point things had gone pretty well, although Beckstead's poll numbers continued to lag. I had tried to convince him that this was going to take many months of sustained effort and some notable successes before those numbers would start to trend back up. That was the last thing he wanted to hear. All he cared about was results and he wanted them right now.

But the essential question—the question which underpinned our every action—the question that nearly a year into his first term remained glaringly unanswered—was this: Does LaGrand Beckstead have what it takes to survive at the top? Is he numbered among the fittest?

IT WAS SEVEN MONTHS after the staff shake-up when a proposal to build a private nuclear waste dump was first raised, causing Beckstead to start salivating like one of Pavlov's dogs. By his estimation, killing the project was a chance to get his lagging job approval numbers back on track. He saw it as the perfect issue on which to define his leadership.

I was suggesting that this may indeed provide the shot in the arm that we needed, but that we should be careful how we approached it. The battle was ours to define, I argued. The Consortium—as we had come to call it—did not want to even admit that there might be grounds for opposing their project. As far as they were concerned, detailing the outlines of a political battle was out of the question. Therefore, we had the power to dictate the rules of engagement. We could define success and failure, and could define success any way we wanted to. But that required patience, a resource on which Beckstead seemed to be eternally running low. No amount of reasoning would slow him down, it seemed. He was determined to charge straight ahead, taking his political future on a complete unknown.

The situation was this:

About a year and a half ago a group of five large power companies from around the country had quietly formed a consortium whose objective was building a nuclear waste storage facility, a high-brow euphemism for a nuke dump. The waste generated by nuclear power plants was stored on the site where it is created and the time was quickly approaching when they would be out of storage space. When that happened, by law, the reactors must be shut down. In other words, the nuclear power industry was slowly but steadily choking on its own waste.

The political problem these companies face is pretty simple—no one wants to be the host of a nuclear waste dump. It doesn't look good in the economic development brochures. Even people without any political or environmental problems with nuclear power recognize the stigma associated with being the host state of such a dump and would fight it to the death. Although Governor Beckstead never said as much to me, I strongly suspected that this was his position. He had no strong opposition to nuclear power; he just did not want his state to be the repository of the industry's waste, especially since Utah has no nuclear power plants.

To solve their problem, the nuclear power industry had decided to follow the path the gambling industry had chosen a few decades before. And that path leads to Indian reservations.

Indian reservations provide an enticing venue for this type of project for two reasons. First, the economic situation of many Indian reservations is so bad with rampant unemployment and critically underfunded programs that almost any kind of outside investment seems attractive. Second, state governments have no authority on an Indian reservation. In the eyes of the law they are in most respects on equal footing with the states and subject only to Federal oversight.

This is enough home rule to keep the State of Utah from having any say in whether or not the proposed nuclear waste dump is constructed in our state. I had tried to impress this reality on the Governor, but he did not want to hear it. There were ways to stop the project, I was sure, but my contention was that we needed to determine a course of action before we started calling press conferences and issuing press releases explaining just how many deaths the proposal was going to die.

"If you promise to kill the project, people expect you to do just that," I told him.

"We'll kill it Sammy my boy, we'll kill it," was his retort and the extent of his plan.

JACK LONGNIGHT was a man of slight build and quiet demeanor, both of which made him seem younger than his 46 years. In many ways, Jack was the opposite of Governor Beckstead. Jack had a relaxed, introspective style that those who don't know him often mistook for meekness. But it didn't take many interactions with Jack to realize that under that placid exterior, he was cagey and incredibly tough-minded. I did not know Jack that well when this whole thing started, but I liked him and I was not looking forward to the political battle which seemed to be looming inevitably ahead.

"How are you Jack?" I said as I entered the lobby.

He looked up from a newspaper, "Fine, just fine," he said, extending his hand.

"I hope you haven't been waiting long."

"No, just a minute or so."

"Let's go on back," I said and began leading him through the wood-paneled hall to the Governor's office.

"Jack, come on in. Its good to see you," Governor Beckstead said as we walked through the door.

"Its nice to see you too, Grand," Jack said as the two shook hands.

"I was sorry to hear about Mary Leapingdeer," the Governor said with genuine concern on his face.

"Thank you. We missed you at her funeral," Jack said.

"I was out of town and didn't hear about it until after. I'm sorry," Beckstead said and shot a frustrated glance at me. "Please have a seat," he added, showing Jack to one of several seats around a small conference table.

"I guess you know why I've asked to meet with you," the Governor said after we were all seated.

"You are concerned about the high unemployment on the reservation?" Jack asked, his face betraying nothing.

"Well, that's always a concern. But I want to talk to you about this nuclear thing."

"What about it?"

"For starters, why are you supporting it?"

"Two reasons, jobs and money, its pretty simple," he said as he leaned back in his chair.

"Maybe the state could help you with that without having to bring in radioactive waste," Beckstead offered.

"I'll ignore for the moment the fact that until this very moment the state of Utah has never yet lifted a finger to help us with either of these problems, and ask instead how is it exactly that you envision helping our reservation?'' Jack was skillfully putting the Governor squarely on the hot seat.

''Well, obviously, Jack, I don't have all the answers right now, but there's got to be a lot of things we can do, if we are willing to work together. Can't we work something out?''

''Maybe there's a billion-dollar business you know of somewhere who would be interested in investing their money on the reservation,'' Jack said as if such were somewhere within the realm of the possible.

''Honestly, Jack I have to say that I don't, but—''

''Governor you—and by 'you' I mean the state of Utah—have allowed toxic and hazardous wastes dumps to virtually surround our reservation. Those are businesses the state licensed knowing full well that they are literally in our backyard,'' he said, holding up his hand to keep the Governor from interrupting. ''Never once did anyone ever check with us to see how we felt about living in a hazardous waste zone. Not once. You created the hazardous waste zone, not us. But now that you have surrounded us with this stuff, you want to slam the door shut on us. I ask you again, what else are we supposed to do?'' Jack was referring to a group of industrial waste companies near the Pishute reservation that had been licensed in the 1980s. The county that is the host of these facilities had, for zoning purposes, created a hazardous waste zone. The Pishute reservation was not actually in the zone, but it was close and Jack's point was well taken.

"You know they're just using you, don't you?" Beckstead said, making a clumsy attempt to change tacks.

"And we are using them," Jack responded calmly.

"Look Jack, all I am saying is, let's work together to find an alternative, that's all," Beckstead said as he folded his arms over his chest, trying desperately to find a graceful way to end the conversation.

"That is why I am here. What do you propose?" Jack said, as though he expected a plan from the governor.

The room fell into an awkward silence as Jack stared at the Governor in order to emphasize his point that there was indeed no alternative plan.

"Well, let's both think about what can be done out there and get together soon," the Governor said, abandoning grace all together and just doing anything he could to bring the meeting to an end.

GRUDGINGLY, I had to admit that Jack had handled the meeting perfectly. I had expected him to launch into a full-scale defense of the nuclear dump, refusing to listen to anything we said. Instead he made it clear that he was more than willing to listen to our plan, knowing full well that we had no way to match the economic and financial incentives the Consortium had put on the table.

For his part, the meeting left Beckstead in the increasingly familiar position of having been outmaneuvered. The frustration in his eyes was easy to read as I escorted Jack from the office. The fact that I had been right about going half-cocked into this meeting only served to make him angrier.

I WALKED JACK TO the front lobby, thanked him for coming and returned to my desk where I found a message from Wayne Smith. Smitty, as he was known to everyone who knew him, had been the political beat reporter for the *Capitol Times* since the time that smoke signals were considered a mass media.

The *Capitol Times* was the largest, most influential newspaper in the state and Smitty was one of the big reasons why that was the case. Legendary for his hard-driving, sharp-witted approach to political reporting, the mere sound of his name caused most politicians to begin reflexively spewing expletives, while hearing the phrase "Smitty's on line four," has, during his decades-long reign of terror, sent the blood pressure of legions of press secretaries soaring to medically dangerous levels. Although in fairness to Smitty, I must admit that no coroner has ever attributed the cause of a fatal heart attack directly to one of Smitty's phone calls. But then again, some people will tell you there is no direct link between smoking cigarettes and cancer either.

I had spent several years on Smitty's rack before I realized that for some reason, which he never explained and I never dared question, he liked me. Unfortunately, his fondness for me did not spill over on any of my employers, none of whom were spared his hammer. In fact, although he denied it, Smitty had taken a strong dislike to Beckstead and spent much of his time and energy focused on his administration. That I maintained a good relationship with Smitty did not sit well with Beckstead. I had tried to convince him that my relationship was a benefit to him, but Beckstead wasn't buying and I did not blame him.

I picked up the phone and returned Smitty's call.

"Smitty," he said when he answered the phone.

"Smitty. Sam. What's up?" When Smitty called, he called on business. Small talk, if there was any, was exchanged at the end of our conversations.

"Yeah Sam, thanks for calling. I, uh, need your help," he said. Smitty does not often need my help and since being in his good graces was akin to a papal dispensation, I always tried to accommodate.

"What can I do for you?"

"I need some information from the San Francisco Police Department," he said and let the request hang there without explanation.

"I don't know how much help I can be with that. I don't know anybody in the San Francisco Police Department," I said after I realized he was not going to say anything else.

"I was thinking you might call the Mayor's office for me," he said.

"Maybe you better give me a better idea about what you need," I said.

There was a brief silence followed by a long exhale on Smitty's end. It was obvious that Smitty was uncomfortable asking me this favor. After all the times he has made me squirm, I was enjoying having the roles reversed.

"Did you know Jeff Leapingdeer was killed in a car crash two weeks ago?" he finally asked me.

I had known of Jeff and we had met maybe once or twice. He had been a lawyer in San Francisco. His mother, Mary Leapingdeer, had been a member of the Pishute Tribal Council until her death about a month before. Well into her eighties when she died, she had taken a nasty fall in her shower where she was found dead a couple of days later.

"I think I heard something about Jeff being killed in an accident, but I thought someone was getting him and his mother confused," I said.

"No, they are both dead and I'm looking into it. What I need is to ask the investigating officer some questions, but because of some inane departmental policy the only person they'll let me talk to is some PR hack. A kid really. Knows absolutely nothing about the wreck. He's just reading to me off the police report which I already have a copy of," he said, the frustration rising in his voice. Reporters think they ought to be able to talk to anybody about anything anytime they want. Smitty was especially spoiled in that regard.

"I'm flattered that you think my vast powers extend to the San Francisco Police Department. But I can't make them change their policy," I said, unable to resist the urge to tease him.

"Of course you can't. But if you called the Mayor's office and asked them to do you, the Governor's Chief of Staff, a favor they might be able to loosen things up," he said.

"I don't know, Smitty."

"Quit jerking me around Sam, you gonna help me or not?" Should Smitty ever need to fill out a resume, I would strongly suggest that he not list "supplication" under his job skills.

"Okay, I'll do it," I said as if I was just as put out as he.

WHAT SMITTY DID not know—and I didn't tell him—was that his request was not that big of a deal. Since I had taken this job with Beckstead, I had developed a friendship with Penny McGriff, Chief of Staff to the California governor. After hanging up with Smitty, I called Penny and told her what I needed. She understood perfectly why I wanted to deliver on Smitty's request. Without making any promises, she said she would call the mayor's office and see what she could do.

Later that afternoon, I got a call back.

"Good news is they'll let you talk to the investigating officer. Bad news is they're not going to let him speak to your reporter friend. They wouldn't budge on that," she said with a finality that ended any thought that they might compromise.

"That'll work just fine I think. Don't worry about

it, thanks for your help. I really appreciate it,'' I said, hoping it would satisfy Smitty.

''No problem at all. I'll see you next week at the NGA meetings,'' she said, referring to the National Governor's Association meetings which were being held in Sacramento the following week.

''I'll be there. Let's have dinner or something,'' I said.

''Sounds like a plan. Look me up when you get here.''

''Thanks Penny. It'll be on me.''

My next call was to Smitty.

''Those pricks,'' he said when I told him what the deal was going to be. Smitty is the kind of person that motivates himself by seeing the whole world as combined in a conspiracy, not to seek his destruction, but simply to dole out little injustices in order to make his life as difficult as possible. This provided further evidence.

''It's the best I can do Smitty, take it or leave it,'' I said.

''I'll take it, I'll take it,'' he said, clearly disgusted with having to rely so heavily on my help. I, on the other hand, was loving it.

''Tell me what you want to know, I'll call the guy first thing in the morning,'' I said.

''Call him? You can't call him, this has to be done in person. You aren't going to learn anything talking to the guy over the phone,'' he said.

''What? You just need some details on an accident,

right? That shouldn't require a personal visit," I said, a little befuddled.

"Maybe we better get together for dinner. You got plans?"

"No. Where do you want to meet?"

"How about Lucky's?" he suggested.

"Lucky's? That's just a bar, isn't it? They don't serve dinner there, do they?" I said. I had never been there and wasn't particularly interested in ever going.

"Yeah, they serve food there. Good food. See you in thirty minutes?"

"Make it an hour, I've got to make sure Alice gets some dinner before I come," I said.

"An hour then."

ALICE IS AN English Bulldog. I got her from the local Bulldog Rescue Society not long after the last election. The first two years of her life were spent with an old man in a single-wide trailer and eleven other of his closest canine friends. The noise, mess and stench finally became too much for the neighbors who called in animal control, who in turn broke up the happy little home. The Bulldog Rescue Society had saved Alice from certain destruction.

Alice is everything you would want in a bulldog—short, white, ugly, fat—excepting one major flaw, she has the strangest temperament of any dog I have ever known. Most dogs adore their owners and are suspicious of strangers. Alice is just the opposite. Every stranger she meets she loves—to her, my neighbors are like family, the plumber and the cable guy are her best friends. Me—she has no use for. I thought for a while that she would grow out of this disposition as she learned to trust me. But she never has and I have had to learn to live with it.

When I'm out of town, she won't be boarded at a dog kennel. I tried it once and she moped around the apartment for weeks afterward, refusing to eat or even acknowledge that I existed. So now when I leave town I pay Daniel, one of the neighborhood kids, to come over twice a day, feed her and take her out for walks. Alice loves Daniel, of course, and prefers that I do a lot of traveling.

When I stopped by that night, on my way to Lucky's, Alice had plopped down by the sliding glass door overlooking my small patio, watching the traffic go by. When I walked in she nodded her head just enough to acknowledge my presence and then went back to traffic monitoring.

"Please, don't get up," I said. "I just stopped by to get your dinner."

Alice didn't budge.

I walked into the kitchen and poured her dog food, which had to be special ordered through the veterinarian, into her bowl and got her some fresh water.

"Dinner is served, my lady. I'll be home in a couple of hours," I said.

She couldn't be bothered.

I walked out of the apartment and shut the door

behind me, as I did I heard Alice make her all-out, lumbering assault on the food bowl.

Sure enough, when I pulled into the parking lot the sign, which I had seen thousands of times driving up and down Main Street but never read said, "Lucky's Bar *and Grill.*" Even a cursory glance at Lucky's would suggest that whatever streak of good fortune its namesake had once been riding had long since given way to hard times. It was a seedy little establishment three times as long as it was wide, with a bar running the entire length of one wall and booths down the other. The back of each booth was tall, reaching almost to the ceiling, making it hard to find Smitty. When I did, he was already nursing a drink. We exchanged hellos as I took the seat opposite him.

"Nice place," I said.

"Won't hurt you to rub elbows with the common folk for an hour or so," he said.

"No, it won't. When do they arrive?" I said with a smile. Smitty could not help but offer a chuckle.

"Hey Lucky, two dinner specials," Smitty yelled to the old man behind the bar. "What you drinking?" he said to me.

"Club soda," I said, knowing he would not like it.

"Come on Sammy, don't embarrass me here in front of my friends," he said.

"Just plain water?" I said hoping that would meet with his approval.

"Another one of these," he said holding up his empty glass. "And a water for Peter Pan here."

Lucky acknowledged the order with a slight nod of his head and walked back toward the kitchen.

"Okay Smitty, you have my attention. What's the big deal?" I said.

"I'm not sure. There may not be a deal at all," he said, obviously having decided to low-key whatever it was that he was working on.

"Well what is it?"

"Mary Leapingdeer took a fall in her shower a month ago and died. Right?"

I nodded.

"Two weeks ago I get a call from her son, Jeff Leapingdeer. Message says he wants to talk to me about his mother's death. He'll call me the next day, but doesn't leave a return number. The next day? No call. So a couple of days go by and I decide to track him down. I make a few calls, find out he's a lawyer for the World Resources Defense League in San Francisco. When I call there, they tell me he died two weeks ago in a car accident. Died the day he left the message," he said.

"You got to be kidding me. What an amazing, sad coincidence," I said.

"That is exactly my point," he said, pointing his chubby finger at me.

"What?"

"You tell me, Sam, what are the chances that something like that just happens? A coincidence," he said.

"I don't know," I said, a little taken aback by what he seemed to be suggesting.

"I don't know either, but those got to be long, long odds," he said.

"What else do you have?" I asked, thinking there had to be something other than a strange coincidence.

"Well there is this nuclear thing on the reservation."

"Yeah?"

"Mary was on the Tribal Council. She's dead. Her son who works for an environmental attorney, obviously opposed to nuclear dumps anywhere, much less on his own reservation—calls me to talk about his mother's death. Now he's dead too," he said.

"There's one problem with this conspiracy theory you're cooking up." I could see by the look on his face that he knew what I was about to say. "Jeff opposed the dump and Mary supported it. She voted for it in the Tribal Council. I've read the transcripts."

"Okay, okay, there are some inconsistencies, that's why I am looking into it," he said.

"So you want me to drop everything and go to San Francisco just to satisfy your curiosity?" I said.

"That's what reporters do, they satisfy their curiosity," he said, taking a long pull on his drink.

"But I'm not a reporter."

"Look Sammy, I know you're going to be in Sacramento next week for the NGA meetings; just take a little side trip to San Francisco and ask a few harmless questions. That's all I need."

"I read the newspaper about Mary's death. The Tribal Police are satisfied that it was an accident," I said.

"Yeah, but when you really pin them down, they can't completely rule out foul play," he said.

"Well I'm sure it's that way with every fatal accident with no witnesses. It's impossible to say for absolute sure what exactly happened," I said.

"Come on, Sammy, give me a break here, I'm just trying to do my job," he said as though he needed to finish sweeping up so he could clock out.

"I don't know Smitty, I'm leaving for Washington, D.C. tomorrow. When I get back from there I got to turn right around and go to Sacramento—this will be another day I've got to be out of the office. The work piles up," I said, facetiously pointing out that this was not exactly a small favor he was asking.

"Why are you busting my chops on this? All I need to know is if you're going to help me or not," said Smitty, ever gracious.

"When you put it like that, Smitty you're impossible to resist."

Like I said, it is always good to have Smitty in your debt.

IF FORCED, I would have to admit that Lucky's meatloaf was the best I had ever tasted. I don't eat meatloaf that often, mind you, but it was good nonetheless. After I had agreed to make the trip to San Francisco to talk to the police officer, Smitty had changed the subject to politics. When I talk politics with Smitty I have to be extremely careful, because whatever I say often finds its way onto the pages of the *Capitol Times*.

On my way home I stopped by Daniel's apartment and gave him the last minute instructions for taking care of Alice while I was in D.C.

"No problem Sam," he said as I slipped a twenty-dollar bill in his hand. "Taking care of Alice is the easiest twenty bucks around."

"I'm glad you think so Daniel. I also wanted to give you this," I said and handed him a key. "I had a key made to my apartment for you. You can keep it. That way we don't have to constantly swap it back and forth."

"Great, that'll make it easier, like if you're going to be working late or something."

I patted him on the back and couldn't resist giving him another twenty bucks as I left.

TWO

WHEN I GOT HOME, Alice was already curled up on her bed in the laundry room and snoring away. I checked my voice mail and found a message from Tracy Harmon.

"Sam, this is Tracey, I'm sorry I missed you. I hope you are still coming to D.C. tomorrow. I haven't heard from you since we made plans to meet for dinner. Anyway, if you are coming I need to push our dinner plans back an hour and instead of meeting at my office, let's just meet at Sequoia at nine o'clock. I hope you're still coming; I need to ask a favor."

Just the sound of her recorded voice made my heart beat a little faster. I had meant to call and reconfirm our plans on several occasions, but it was impossible to catch Tracey at her desk, and I hated leaving voice mails for her. It was already too late tonight to be calling back east, so I called her office phone and left a message on her voice mail apologizing for not calling sooner and confirming the change in our plans.

A LITTLE OVER a year ago, in my resignation letter to Senator Maggie Hansen, I listed several reasons for my decision to leave her staff. But there was one central issue which went unnoted, and that reason could be summed up in two words: Tracey Harmon.

Shortly after taking over as the Senator's Chief of Staff, I needed to hire a communications director. Tracey came highly recommended. She was very impressive in the interview and had all the right qualifications, so I hired her for the job.

Tracey and I worked closely together on the Senator's staff for over two years. For the first year it was a normal business relationship. We saw each other at the office and worked together as the situation called for. But as we did, it became apparent that Tracey understood politics and how to maneuver in a political world. Gradually, I began to rely more and more on her judgement and we found ourselves working together closely. As we did, a friendship developed between us.

When it came time for the Senator's reelection, we both took leaves of absence from the senate staff and moved back to Utah to run the campaign. Looking back on it now, I realize that my decision to move her from the senate staff to the campaign, at least on a subconscious level, had been partially motivated by my personal feelings toward her. But I would not realize that until later.

One evening Tracey and I were working in the campaign headquarters, the only two who had not left for the day. She was in her office, I in mine. She had been working on a press release for the next day's news cycle and came into my office to run the latest draft by me. I was at my desk attempting to wade through a memo forwarded to me by someone on the senate staff. She handed me the release and stood behind me looking over my shoulder as I read through it.

When I finished reading it she leaned over my shoulder and started pointing to the release, explaining how she planned to move this bit of text here, move that there, change this word, etc. But as she did, I caught a lingering scent of her perfume. It caught me a little off guard, almost startling me. She continued to talk about the release, but I couldn't be bothered with it. I was mesmerized by the way the muscles in her jaw rippled as she spoke, the way she delicately, thoughtlessly brushed her hair behind her ear and away from her clear brown eyes, the way she was completely unaware of how she had captivated me at the moment, the way her face was purposeful, yet allowed a smile to peek through every few moments.

Then she stopped talking and turned her face toward me. I looked back for several seconds with some silly look on my face before I realized she was waiting on a reply from me. The grin fell quickly from my face, replaced by a bright red sheen as I stumbled around for something to say. I had no idea what a correct response to her question would be, so I finally just agreed with what she had been suggesting and hoped for the best.

That moment had been the beginning of the end of my tenure with Senator Maggie Hansen. When the campaign ended and the fanfare died down, I quietly submitted my resignation and recommended that Tracey be hired as my replacement.

But to my disappointment a relationship with Tracey had not bloomed as I had hoped. At one time, I had sensed in Tracey a willingness to test the relationship to see if there might be something more to it than a friendship. But by the time I was in a situation where I felt like I could pursue a relationship with Tracey, we had already settled into a very comfortable friendship, which had now taken on a certain inertia.

By the time I moved back to Wasatch City, we had become close friends and were spending a lot of time together. But the time for taking the next step never seemed right. Looking back on it now, I realize I missed a lot of good opportunities waiting for the perfect opportunity to come around.

Shortly after I left D.C., Tracey started seeing other people again, causing me to spend many idle moments wondering if she was dating because a friendship was all she wanted from me or because I had never given her a reason not to see other people. Whether or not she was aware of the anxiety this caused me I can't say for certain, but if she was, she was considerate in her handling of the situation. If weekend plans came up in the course of a conversation she would offhandedly mention that she was going to dinner with a friend or she'd been asked to a play at the Kennedy Center or whatever the case may have been.

Then one evening several weeks back, I had called

her apartment in D.C. and the phone was answered by a man. When Tracey came on the line, she was warm and friendly as always and cheerfully explained that she was just headed out for the evening.

Although I had been in denial of it for several months, hearing another man answer her phone served as a wake-up call of sorts. Tracey's dating schedule, I realized, was becoming somewhat crowded and whatever my window of opportunity may have been, it was now closing with increasing momentum.

The next morning I made a brief appearance at the office for a staff meeting, noting with some pride that the team I had assembled for Governor Beckstead had pulled together rather nicely and was beginning to be not only efficient but also incredibly effective at what they did. When it was almost too late, I hustled out the door to make a 10:05 flight to Dulles International Airport in Washington, making the flight with 10 minutes to spare. The flight arrived on schedule at 4:10.

The reason for my trip was to attend the first scheduled meeting of the Nuclear Regulatory Commission—or as it is more commonly known, the NRC—regarding the nuclear dump proposal. I had been assured by the lawyers in our Attorney General's office that this first meeting was simply a lot of pro forma stuff. However, there was just enough petty political jealousy between the Governor's and the Attorney General's office that I felt obliged to monitor the situation for myself. Besides, it did provide a coveted chance to see Tracey.

Once on the ground I caught a cab up to Capitol Hill and renewed friendships with some of my former colleagues. In doing so, I paid a visit to an old friend of mine who was the Chief of Staff to the Senate Finance Committee. An idea for killing the project had been percolating in the back of my mind for several weeks and I wanted to run it by her. The Consortium, I thought, might be stopped dead in their tracks by a one-sentence rider to the NRC budget stating that none of the money appropriated could be used for the nuclear dump docket. She liked the idea and promised her help if it was needed.

The problem with this plan was that Senator Hansen would have to carry the water on it and would therefore be the hero. Which was just fine with me, other than the fact that Beckstead had made it absolutely clear that he wanted to deal the deathblow himself while bathed in the adulation of a grateful constituency. But, just in case that was not possible, I thought I'd better have a back-up plan.

IT WAS AFTER 7:00 p.m. when I left Capitol Hill and hopped a cab to Georgetown. I had it drop me at the end of K Street where it dead-ends into the left bank of the Potomac. To me, the Potomac is one of the most beautiful rivers flowing through an urban setting anywhere in the world. And the plaza where the restaurant Sequoia is set is one of my favorite places in D.C. From the quaint but life-like statues that dot the plaza, to the meandering pace of the river as it makes an obtuse bend, it is an idyllic setting for a restaurant and the perfect venue for capping off a D.C. day.

Arriving a little before 8:00, I tried strolling around the plaza for a while but the heat and humidity forced me to the sanctuary of Sequoia's central air conditioning. I found a seat at the bar and sipped a club soda while waiting for my table to become available. A few minutes before 9:00, a gaunt-looking hostess found me at the bar and showed me to my table, walking and pouting as though she were sauntering down a Paris runway. Judging by her emaciated condition and the total contempt she held for the restaurant's clientele, I could not imagine why she wasn't.

Reaching a cozy table for two overlooking the Potomac, she turned and gave me her I'm-smiling-now-only-because-I-have-to smile and said, "Will this do?"

"Yes, nicely," I responded to myself since the hostess was, by then, already halfway back to her station.

Sequoia is a big spacious restaurant, with extremely high ceilings and an ambiance to match. My table was not only perfectly situated for enjoying the dinner and a stunning view, but also provided an excellent location for watching the restaurant's entrance. As I waited, my heart rate began a slow crescendo. It was the entrance, not the stunning view that was captivating my attention.

A few minutes after 9:00, she arrived.

Walking in the door, she stopped and spoke to the

hostess who directed her toward the restrooms, into which Tracey disappeared. Moments later my breath caught in my chest as she emerged. Her blond hair which had been pulled up and back, now fell around her shoulders, her business suit was sans a coat and a few other minor adjustments had been changed to more alluring evening attire.

After hanging the coat on a nearly barren coat rack, she began surveying the restaurant for me. A smile leapt to her face as she picked me out of the crowd and winked at me. The picture of her making her way to me across the crowded restaurant is not one I will soon forget. The light of dusk was gradually giving way to flickering candlelight, her hair bouncing, swaying on her shoulders, her gaze fixed on me, her left leg peeking evasively through a slit in her skirt.

I rose to greet her.

"It is so nice to see you, Sam. Sorry I'm late," she said as she placed a small, black handbag on the table, delicately taking both of my hands in hers, leaning over and not quite kissing me on the cheek.

"Please, don't mention it. Have a seat," I said as I pulled back her chair.

"I'm glad you could make it. I worried that you wouldn't when you didn't call," she said.

"I'm sorry about that. I hate leaving voice mails."

"No matter. You made it," she said, her smiling eyes signaling her willingness to forgive my breech of etiquette.

"Its good to see you. You look...beautiful," I said trying to be gracious but not effusive and failing.

"Thank you. It's been a hectic day, I came straight here from the Justice Department. Nice to relax a bit," she said.

"I've been hanging out on your stomping ground, catching up with some people I haven't seen in a while."

"You were on the Hill?" she asked.

"Yeah, for a couple of hours."

"Did you stop by and see the Senator?"

"No. I meant to but I got caught up with other things," I lied. I didn't stop by because Tracey had asked to meet here and I thought there might have been a reason she did not want me to come by her office.

"She won't be very happy when she finds out that her Boy Wonder came all the way to Capitol Hill and didn't stop by," she said in mock concern.

"Maybe it's best if she doesn't find out," I suggested facetiously.

"Can't you stop by before you leave town? Seriously, I know she would like to see you," she said.

"My day is pretty tight tomorrow, but I'll try," I said.

"How's the Governor doing?" she asked.

"He's fine. But let's not talk shop tonight. That's all we ever do when we're together," I said.

"I don't know. What else is there besides work?" she said, alluding to the fact that a Capitol Hill chief of staff works an average of seventy hours a week.

Just then the waiter arrived to take our order. Tracey ordered a pine nut and duck dumpling dish and I ordered scampi on angel hair.

"What kind of interesting hikes have you been on lately?" she asked as the waiter retreated.

"You know, I haven't been since that day you and I hiked up to Mirror Lake," I said.

"You have got to be kidding me. That was over a year ago," she said. The reality of the statement surprised both of us.

"Over a year," I said allowing myself a moment to remember a portrait of her sitting by the lake that day.

"It was...breathtaking. I can't believe you haven't been again," she said, bringing me back to Sequoia.

"What can I say, I'm busy too," I said in my defense.

"If I lived out there, I would be out on some trail every weekend," she said, and knowing Tracey I had no reason to doubt it.

"I'm sure of it. Let's plan on going the next time you're in town," I suggested.

"Let's do," she said as if it were a done deal, but offered no further details on when she might actually be in Wasatch City.

It was then that I thought about asking about the favor she had mentioned in her message, but took a decision against it, thinking that it might bring us back to shop talk. It was best, I decided, to let her choose the timing.

A few minutes later our salads arrived. We continued to exchange small talk throughout the evening, both of us struggling at times to avoid work topics. Except for a few awkward moments, it was a great evening.

The entire evening passed without mention of a favor.

THREE

THE NEXT MORNING I took the D.C. Metro blue line to Rockville, Maryland where the Nuclear Regulatory Commission was located. I didn't really expect to learn a whole lot at this first meeting, but since it was going to be such a big issue for the Governor I felt compelled to be in attendance.

In all my years in Washington with Senator Hansen I had never had occasion to do business with the NRC. The meeting was just as it had been advertised by our Attorney General's office—pro forma. With the added dimension of being mind-numbingly tedious.

I spent the morning and the first part of the afternoon fighting off a nap and trying my best to pay attention to what was going on. Without haste the commission moved through its docket, no detail too small to be exhaustively dealt with, no objections—no matter how trivial—unconsidered. I had been warned that the issues of real substance would be considered in later meetings, and I assumed that was when the sparks would fly.

Finally, after discussing every possible inconsequential issue that could come up, the chairman dropped his gavel and adjourned the session. The elation of leaving the dentist chair after a long-dreaded double root canal could not match my mood as I finally walked out of the Commission chambers.

"You must be Mr. McKall," a well-dressed man in a dark blue suit said as I made my way to the front door.

"Yes. And you are?" I asked as we shook hands.

"Tom Griggs. I'm the project coordinator for Waste Solutions."

Waste Solutions Inc. was the name under which the Consortium was doing business. I liked calling it the "The Consortium"; it sounded more sinister.

"Nice to finally meet you, Tom," I said.

"It looks as though we may be seeing a lot of each other," he said with a grin that was a little too forced.

"It does appear that way."

"Not only because of this," he said, pointing his thumb over his shoulder toward the Commission chamber. "I just rented a house in Wasatch City, in what I believe you call 'the Avenues'," he continued, blissfully unaware that he had moved in to Utah's hotbed of environmental fervor.

I suppressed a laugh and said, "That's nice, welcome to Utah."

"Thank you. It looks like we're getting together next week as well," he said.

"Really?"

"Yeah, I called your office a few days ago and made an appointment with Governor Beckstead. I assume you'll be there," he said, enjoying the fact that he was telling me something I should have already known. Neither Beckstead nor the scheduler had bothered to tell me that he had called.

"I've been out of the office, so I'm not completely up to speed," I said, putting the best face I could on it.

"I know how that is. Listen, we want to work with you on this project," he said and earnestly furrowed his brow as he waited for my response.

"I don't really know if that's going to be possible, Tom. I don't see much room for compromise," I said.

"You guys are looking at this the wrong way. It doesn't have to be a zero sum game. I mean, there's a lot of money behind this project and there is no reason why some of it shouldn't go to the state of Utah," he said.

These people were smart. I had to give them that. A less sophisticated approach would have been to try and bully their way through the process, never stopping to consider whether any of our objections had merit or not. Under this scenario, it would have been much easier to cast them in the role of the soulless, faceless corporation. But the offer of money was an implied recognition that our concerns may be legitimate and demonstrated a willingness to compensate us for them.

The offer itself would change things significantly. If done in the right way, targeted toward the right programs and groups, it could very well win them a support base inside the state; people willing to overlook the stigma of a nuclear dump in order to advance their agenda. In politics, divide and conquer is almost never a bad strategy.

This was the worst news of the day.

"I wouldn't get your hopes up. I think the Governor has made up his mind," I said.

"That may be true, but don't underestimate the power of the checkbook to enlighten the mind," he said, knowing exactly where the strength of his proposal lay.

I DIDN'T HAVE TIME to pay Senator Hansen a visit; in fact, I barely made it to my flight. It was, however, uneventful, getting me back to Wasatch City just after 9:00. Before going to my apartment I drove by the office, shuffled some papers and checked my phone messages. Then I headed to my apartment, stopping long enough to pick up a sandwich.

At home there was a note from Daniel taped to my refrigerator.

Sam,
Alice and I broke the vase on the end table in your bedroom. She knocked it off when she was fetching one of her chew toys.
Sorry, Daniel

Fetching a chew toy? I have never been able to get Alice to fetch. After unpacking my things I found a message from Tracey on my voice mail.

"Sam, this is Tracey, I guess you didn't have time to drop by this afternoon. That's okay, I know you were busy. I still have a favor to ask, I should have asked last night, but...anyway, will you call me at the office tomorrow? Have someone find me if I don't answer my phone. Thanks again for dinner, I really enjoyed it. Talk to you soon.''

Hanging up the phone, I was very curious as to what this favor could be. I mulled it over twice as long as any rational person would have before giving up and turning on CNN to catch up on what was happening in the world. I watched the news, read for a couple hours and turned in for the evening.

I made it into the office at about 7:00 the next morning and read the *Capitol Times* until about 8:00 before picking up the phone to call Tracey.

''Hi Tracey, Sam. I got your message last night,'' I said when she picked up her phone.

''Sam. Thanks for calling back. How are you?''

''Good. How are you?''

''Good... Good. How was your flight?''

''Uneventful.''

''That's good.''

There was an awkward pause as I waited for her to pick up the conversation by asking her favor.

''Listen, great. I need to ask you a favor,'' she said, almost stuttering over her words. I had never known her to be this way.

''Sure,'' I said.

''Do you have plans over Labor Day?''

''Nothing definite.'' I had nothing at all, but I did not want to sound too pathetic.

''Good,'' she said, almost relieved. This was

strange behavior indeed for Tracey, who was usually very confident and straightforward. "My family. You know my family?...In Maine?"

"Yes."

"They... We always have a sort of an end-of-the-summer get together over Labor Day weekend," she said and paused as if it were my turn to speak.

"That must be a lot of fun," I said.

"Yes, it's a lot of fun. But you know, everyone's married. All my brothers and sisters. I'm the last one and I hate showing up every year alone. I'll pay for your plane ticket and everything, but if you can't make it, I know it is short notice," she said.

That's the thing about Tracey. Just when I had begun preparing myself emotionally for things not to work out between us, she comes back at me with something like this.

I could tell it had been hard for her to work up to asking me and, as a joke, I thought about telling her I'd have to get back to her. But that was just too mean.

"Sounds like a lot of fun. I'll look forward to it," I said.

"Great, great," she said, but then added, "I'll owe you a huge favor for this one." Which was just enough to keep me wondering whether or not she asked me as a favor or out of some other interests. The whole thing was simultaneously baffling and intriguing.

"Don't mention it," I finally blurted out.

"I'll send you a ticket."

"Don't worry about it, I'll just cash in some miles. I have over a million," I said.

"No I insist, you're doing me a favor."

"No seriously, it will be fine. But just one question," I said.

"Okay."

"Why didn't you ask me this the other night?" I asked not willing to let her completely off the hook.

"I planned to. But...I don't know...it didn't come up."

"What do you mean, 'it didn't come up'? Were you hoping I'd invite myself?" I said, having a good laugh at her expense.

"A real gentleman would have," she said, trying to act as though she did not also find it amusing.

"Believe me, had I known this is what you wanted, I would have," I said, hoping the implication of it was not lost in the moment.

I HUNG UP the phone as confused as ever about Tracey, but with an invitation to spend the weekend with her family. That was good. Right?

FOUR

IT WAS LATE on Wednesday afternoon the following week when we finished the NGA meetings in Sacramento. I was tired and wishing I had not committed to becoming the enabler of Smitty's paranoid fantasies. A desk piled high with work and a voice mail full of messages waited for me in Wasatch City. I thought briefly about calling Smitty with an excuse, but I had committed to drive to San Francisco and meet with the police and I realized that if I backed out now, he would never forgive me.

So just after dark I rented a car at my hotel in Sacramento and headed west on Interstate 80 to San Francisco. It was an easy drive and I arrived at my hotel shortly after 9:00.

"I have a message for you, Mr. McKall," the clerk said as he finished checking me in. "It's from a Mr. Smith, says he will meet you in the bar." Using his whole hand rather than just his index finger, he pointed in the direction of the bar.

At first I didn't understand who he was referring to. But then it dawned on me, Smitty had come over from Wasatch City. I sent my things up to the room with a bellboy and walked over to the bar.

It was your typical hotel bar with pseudo-bamboo furniture and glass-top tables with cheesy standup drink menus flecked with dried-up buffalo wing sauce. It was mostly empty except for the occasional traveling salesman, trying to drink up the courage to face one more soulless hotel room. Smitty, woefully out of place in such an upscale establishment, had tucked himself into the darkest available corner and covered his flanks with several empty tumblers.

"What are you doing here?" I said as I approached his table.

"Never send a boy to do a man's job," he said as he reached over and pulled out a chair for me to sit.

"Thanks for the vote of confidence," I said as I took my seat.

"You said it yourself, Sammy. At Lucky's. You are no reporter."

"Smitty, you do understand I can't take you with me to this meeting tomorrow?" I said.

"I have to," he said emphatically.

"You can't. Absolutely not. That was the deal I made with the Governor's Chief of Staff," I said just as emphatically.

"Once we're there, they're not going to care who you bring," he said.

"No, Smitty, they will care. You know as well as I do, that if the PR guy is any good at all he'll be in the meeting. Believe me he knows what the ground rules are. If I show up with a reporter he'll just shut the whole thing down. And you won't get any questions answered."

"Don't tell 'em I'm a reporter."

"There's not a press secretary in this country that couldn't pick you out of a line-up as a reporter, Smitty. Just look at yourself. You may as well go in there wearing a fedora hat with a card that says 'Press' stuck in the band."

"All right, all right. You win," he said as though he was making a concession to me.

"Why don't we go over what you want me to ask," I said.

"Okay, listen. What you want to do is just get him talking about the accident. Don't ask a lot of questions until he tells you everything he knows off the top of his head. Then pry into any detail that seems odd or out of place. Anything that doesn't add up. Find out how extensively they investigated it. Where the car is now. What was in the car when they found it. Did they ever consider foul play? I guarantee you, if it was a murder, something won't fit and you've got to find it. This may be our only shot," he said.

"First of all, that's a big 'if.' Second, I am only here as a favor to you, I am not investigating anything," I said.

"That right there," he said, raising his index finger from his glass and pointing at me, "that attitude, is the reason I came all the way out here. You go in there with that attitude and anything they say that might be helpful is going in one ear and out the other. To do this right, you've got to be suspicious of everything. Question every assumption, examine every angle, dispute every fact. You got to do that. Got to. Or this will be a waste of time for both of us."

I was already feeling like that was going to be the case no matter how I performed in the meeting.

"I'll do my best, Smitty," I said and patted him on his hand much as the way you would to assure a 90-year-old lady that everything was going to be all right. The humor of it was lost on Smitty.

AFTER MY USUAL fitful night of hotel sleep, Smitty and I met for breakfast in the hotel restaurant and then caught a cab to the San Francisco PD Headquarters, arriving a few minutes before the appointed time. I left Smitty on a bench in front of the building and headed in.

I was shuffled from one receptionist to another, until finally shown into a small interrogation room sparsely decored with a small metal table and four chairs, two on each side. The walls were two tone, both dull shades of gray.

"Wait here," said a white-haired uniformed officer and left without any further explanation.

Within a minute or two another police officer and man about ten years my junior in a tan suit entered the room.

"Mr. McKall, I am Dane Felton. This is Officer Shultz," the man in the suit was saying. "I am an assistant to the Director of Communications for the San Francisco Police department and Lt. Shultz was the investigating officer on the accident you are concerned with. How can we help you?"

"Thank you, it's nice to meet you," I said as I stood and shook their hands.

"Please have a seat," Felton said.

"Thank you for taking the time to meet with me. I'm sure this is a major inconvenience for you." I paused so that they could tell me how glad they were to help and that this was really no problem. Neither man said a word, so I continued.

"Officer Shultz," I turned my attention completely on the uniformed officer, "A couple of weeks ago you investigated an accident that killed Jeff Leapingdeer."

"That is correct," Shultz spoke very carefully as if he were testifying in court.

"Can you tell me about it?" I asked.

"Certainly. We received a call about 00:15 hours, that's 12:15 a.m., reporting an accident on Panoramic Highway."

"Panoramic Highway is a steep winding road that goes up to the top of Mt. Tamalpais. It's a major mountain biking area about 20 miles north of here. Not the kind of road you want to be drinking and driving on," Felton interjected.

"That's right, it's a dangerous road," Shultz agreed and resumed his account of what happened.

I was dispatched and arrived on the scene at approximately 00:30 hours. I found Mr. Leapingdeer's car overturned and in flames. The fire department, which had arrived a few minutes after me, began putting the fire out. Mr. Leapingdeer died in the crash. From the skid marks on the road, I determined that

Mr. Leapingdeer was traveling in excess of 80 miles an hour when he left the road and rolled five times down a sixty-three-foot embankment.

"After the fire was out we discovered two liquor bottles. One inside the car and the other had been thrown from the car as it rolled down the hill. Both bottles were empty. Given the high rate of speed and that he was clearly not in control of his vehicle, we determined that Mr. Leapingdeer was probably intoxicated at the time of the accident.

"When we attempted to notify his next of kin I learned that his mother had recently died." At this point the officer shrugged his shoulders and raised his eyebrows as if to say, "It's pretty obvious why he was drinking, isn't it?"

"Autopsy was inconclusive on how much alcohol was actually in his system. The body was too badly burned. I found absolutely no evidence of foul play. The guys at forensics examined the car and came to the same conclusion. It's a pretty straightforward DUI. Frankly we're just lucky Mr. Leapingdeer did not kill anyone else," the officer said, turning the palms of his hand up and nodding as if to say, "Not much of a story, but I'm done."

"Do you know if Mr. Leapingdeer had ever been arrested or cited for a DUI before?" I asked, not sure where to begin.

"Yes, I looked into that, but there had been no prior arrests or convictions," the officer said.

"It's common for this type of thing to happen to someone going through an emotional trauma such as

Mr. Leapingdeer was. We see it all the time," Felton quickly added.

"That's true," the officer concurred.

"Is that a statistic that is tracked by your department or is it based on experience?" I asked, fishing for anything.

"It's not an official number, it just seems to happen a lot," Felton said.

"Did you talk to anyone who had been with him or talked to him earlier that night?" I asked.

"I talked to several of his co-workers. They said he stayed late at work that evening. Apparently he had just returned from his mother's funeral in Utah and they thought he was catching up on some work. As far as I could tell, they were the last people to see him alive," the officer said.

"He was not married. Correct?" I said.

"That is correct."

"Any significant other?"

"Not that I am aware of," the officer said as he shifted in his seat.

"Is that something you investigated?"

"Not aggressively," the officer said. I took that to mean "no."

"If the autopsy was inconclusive about blood alcohol levels, how are you so sure the bottles of liquor were consumed?"

"First of all, the autopsy did find alcohol in the blood system, they just couldn't get an accurate reading on the level. Second, neither bottle had a lid, strongly suggesting that they were empty at the time of the crash. The bottle that landed outside the vehicle still had a wet residue inside the bottle when I arrived on the scene. And third, he had lost control of the vehicle. That adds up pretty clearly, in my mind at least, to a DUI,'' the officer said.

''Is there any chance that the accident was caused by a brake failure?'' I asked and the officer immediately brightened as if he were extremely proud of what he was about to say.

''Judging by the thick black skid marks left on the road, I would have to say that the brakes were working just fine at the time of the accident. But if that's not enough for you, when I did the background check on Mr. Leapingdeer, I discovered that three weeks before he had been involved in an accident due to a brake problem. I called the insurance company and found out where his car had been serviced, called the shop and confirmed with the mechanic that Mr. Leapingdeer's brakes were completely new and sound,'' he said.

''Well it certainly appears to be a pretty straightforward DUI,'' I said.

''That is what we thought, too. May we ask why you are so interested in Mr. Leapingdeer?'' the PR man said.

''His mother was a very important person in the Pishute Tribe of Indians in Utah,'' I said.

''I understand that, but I could have told you everything Officer Shultz has just told you. Why the call from the Mayor's office?'' he said, clearly perturbed by the whole thing.

"Listen, I'm sorry. I'm just trying to do a favor for a reporter. I'm sure you understand what I mean," I said, knowing full well he did.

"I suppose so," he said as he stood to shake my hand.

"Thank you for accommodating me, you've been very helpful. Hopefully, I can return the favor some time," I said as we shook hands.

"It's no problem," the officer said. "Glad to help."

I FOUND SMITTY right where I had left him. He jumped up from his seat the moment I emerged from the police station.

"Well?" he said.

"I got to say Smitty, it looks like a pretty straightforward DUI."

"See. See. I knew I should have never let you go in there by yourself," Smitty said, throwing his hand up in the air and turning his back on me.

"Smitty, it's not my fault that the guy had too much to drink and killed himself in a car accident. It happens," I said, feeling more defensive than I should have.

"Alright. Just sit down and go over with me word for word what was said in there. Don't leave anything out."

We returned to the bench he had been sitting on and I meticulously went over every word and, even though he was frustrated that there wasn't more to go on, Smitty reluctantly seemed satisfied that I had done a "pretty good" job.

"So what do you think?" I asked.

"They never tried to track down a girlfriend?" he said.

"That was the impression I got."

"Well, that will be our first question at the World Resources Defense Fund," he said.

"Excuse me," I said.

"Yeah, I'm going over to talk to his co-workers. You got nothing better to do. Why not come with me?" he said.

"I don't know Smitty. Why should—"

"Aw, shut up and come on. You might learn something."

FIVE

It was about 11:00 a.m. when we got out of the cab in downtown San Francisco in front of the offices of the World Resources Defense Fund. It was one of the newer buildings in town and had that distinctive San Francisco look about it. I followed Smitty through the front door and over to the building directory. He found the office number and we headed for the elevator, but we were stopped by a security guard who required that we sign in and that he call ahead to make sure it was okay for us to go up. It was, and after signing in the guard let us up.

"Who are we meeting with here?" I asked in the elevator.

"Guy by the name of Max Reeve. Friend of Jeff's," he said as the elevator opened to a stylish yet conservative office, fronted by dark-haired, dark-complected woman in her early twenties behind a receptionist desk.

"May I help you gentlemen?" she asked in an English accent as we approached the desk.

"Yes, I'm Wayne Smith and we're here for a meeting with Max Reeve," Smitty said. The secretary then looked at me. It took a moment before I realized that she wanted my name as well.

"Yes, and I'm Sam McKall," I said. After which she picked up the phone to announce that we were here. She then invited us to have a seat in the small waiting area in front of her desk, which we did.

We had only just sat down when a very striking woman walked to the room.

"Mr. Smith?" she said as we arose from our chairs.

"Hello," Smitty said.

"I'm Maxine Reeve," she said as she extended her hand. Smitty like me was a little taken aback—with a name like Max, we had both been expecting a man. But other than her nearly six feet of height, there was nothing masculine about Max Reeve.

"Oh, yes. I'm Wayne Smith," he said, shaking her hand a little too hardily. "And this is my associate Sam McKall."

"Very nice to met you, Ms. Reeve," I said, having had a second longer to overcome the shock.

"Please call me Max. Let's go back to my office," she said and walked out of the foyer the same way she had walked in.

Her office, which was about halfway down the hall, was a mirror image of her, the picture of grace. From the furniture to the expensive art on the wall, it was all, including the occupant—especially the occupant—very beautiful.

"Please have a seat," she said, directing us to a

large leather sofa while she took a seat in an adjacent chair.

"Now, what can I do for you?" she asked when everyone was seated.

"First of all, let me thank you for taking the time to meet with us today," Smitty said.

"Jeff Leapingdeer was one of my dearest friends. I'm happy to see that your paper is interested in doing a story on him," she said. Smitty stole a glance at me to see if I caught the little deception he had used to set this meeting up with Max.

"Ms. Reeve, I don't want to alarm you, but I am looking into the remote possibility that Jeff's death may not have been an accident."

"A suicide?" she asked, a mixture of shock and disbelief on her face.

"No, no. Not suicide, either," he said and paused to let his meaning sink in.

"You mean murdered? You think Jeff may have been murdered?" she said.

"Are you aware that his mother died in an accident a week or so before his crash?" Smitty asked, avoiding a direct answer to her question.

"Yes, of course, he was very broken up by it. I assumed that is why he was out drinking that night. He had only just returned from the funeral," she said.

"Was Jeff a heavy drinker?" Smitty asked.

"I didn't spend much time with Jeff socially. At business lunches he never drank, even when others were. But at office parties, occasionally he'd have something," she said.

"Did he drink a lot at these office parties?"

"Oh no. Almost nothing," she said definitively.

"Were you at all surprised when the police said he was driving drunk?" Smitty said.

"It made it seem much more tragic, like there was a whole other side of Jeff I didn't know," she said. I noticed her eyes becoming glassy. She blinked a few times and took a deep breath.

"Can you explain what you mean by that?" Smitty said. I had never seen this side of him. There was a gentleness to the way he approached Max that I had never seen Smitty use before.

"Well, as I've said, I didn't think Jeff was a heavy drinker. He didn't seem to be reckless. He was always in control. So much so that it was unnerving to people," she said.

"How so?"

"Well, in pressure situations, say a tough negotiation, it didn't seem to have any effect on him. Others would be up and yelling at each other. Jeff would sit calmly by, unfazed. Waiting for his chance. When it came, he calmly and confidently took it. It unnerves most people to deal with someone who never for a second loses his self-control. Jeff knew that and used it to his advantage," she said.

"Maybe he was wound too tight and just snapped," I said.

"I suppose it's possible. But don't misunderstand me. He wasn't the strong silent type, so to speak. He could laugh, joke, relax—he just didn't crack under pressure, that's all."

"Did he have a girlfriend?" Smitty asked.

"I think so," she said.

"You're not sure?" Smitty asked.

"Well, Jeff and I, we used to, you know, flirt a lot around the office. It never developed into anything. But I don't know...I've never tried to put it into words...I guess a mild infatuation between us. Maybe that's not the right word, but you get my point. I'm sure he sensed the same thing. So we never talked much about who we were dating. But I think he was seeing a woman named Sara, pretty seriously," she said. It never ceases to amaze me what Smitty can get people to tell him.

"You could probably find the number in his phone messages," she added.

"Phone messages?" Smitty asked.

"Yes, he kept a month or so of old messages on his desk. If she ever called the office a message would likely be in that stack," she said.

"Is his office still intact?" I asked.

"Yes. There are plenty of people around here who want it. It's been a few weeks now so I don't expect it to be unoccupied much longer," she said.

"And it would be alright if we took a look around in there?" Smitty asked.

"I don't see why not," she said.

"Thank you. Did Jeff ever say anything to you about a nuclear waste dump being proposed in Utah, or mention a company called Waste Solutions, Incorporated?"

"Yes, of course, he was very much opposed to it.

He was trying to persuade the Defense Fund to spend some of its money to fight the dump," she said.

"How likely is it that the World Resources Defense Fund will spend some of its money fighting this dump?" I asked, thinking something good might come out of this trip after all.

"Frankly, it is more likely now. I think we will end up doing it now. As a sort of memorial to Jeff."

"Did he ever talk to you about his mother's involvement with the project?" Smitty asked.

"Oh yes. Like I said, Jeff was always in control of his emotions, but I could tell his mother's support of that project was a major concern to him. Once, I was in his office when he took a call from his mother and they got into a conversation about it. Of course I could only hear his side of the conversation and Jeff was very deferential to her, but it was obvious that there was some disagreement between them," she said.

"Did he ever explain what the disagreement was?"

"He said that his mother was on the tribal council and planned to support the project because the reservation needed the jobs and the money it would provide. She justified her support because it's only supposed to be a temporary site," she said.

Waste Solutions Inc. had been trying to convince everyone that their project was only a temporary site and that once the Federal government got its site open at Yucca Mountain, Nevada, all the waste from the reservation site would be moved there and the site shut down. Anybody with any brains knows that once that waste has made its way to Utah, it's never moving again. The political temptation in Congress and the federal bureaucracies to simply leave it put would be much too great.

"Was he angry with his mother?" Smitty asked.

"Oh no. I would not use the word angry. Frustrated yes, very frustrated. But he was always very, very respectful of his mother. Very deferential to her. It was one of his most endearing qualities," Max said with a kind of distant smile on her face suggesting that she was remembering such a moment.

"Jeff was in a previous accident a couple weeks ago; what can you tell me about that?" Smitty said.

"There's not much to tell really. His brakes failed and he rammed one of those big SUVs from behind at a stoplight. The other car wasn't damaged, but his was. Told me he pushed his brakes, they caught for a second but then sort of gave way and the pedal went straight to the floor. He just rammed into the back of a Suburban, I think it was," she said.

"Do you know where he got his car repaired?" Smitty asked as he looked over at me to let me know that this was one of the questions I forgot to ask the police officer.

"No, I don't believe he ever mentioned that to me, he just said there was a lot of damage."

"Is there anything I haven't asked you about Jeff's death that seems strange or out of place to you?" Smitty said.

"I can't think of anything right now, but I'll call

you if I do. Would you like to see his office now?'' she asked as she stood from her chair.

Jeff's office was only a few doors down from Max's.

''I've got a conference call I need to be on. Would you mind terribly showing yourselves out when you're done in here?'' she asked as we filed into the office.

''No, not at all, Ms. Reeve. Thanks again,'' Smitty said, apparently unable to call her Max.

''Please don't mention it. I am very interested to know how your investigation turns out. Keep me posted won't you,'' she said.

''My pleasure,'' Smitty said and anyone could see that it was.

Jeff's office was slightly smaller than Max's but it was a corner office with a beautiful view of the San Francisco skyline. It was a pleasant space with an executive table rather than desk, a long credenza and leather chairs, but not as precisely planned as her office.

From the looks of the office everything was pretty much as he had probably left it. The desk, while not perfectly straight, was neat nonetheless. Like Max's office, there were two guest chairs positioned in front of his desk and a sofa, chair, and coffee table tucked into a corner. On the table were magazines ranging from law journals to *Smithsonian*.

Smitty headed straight for the stack of messages piled in a small leather-box on the corner of his desk.

''Several messages in here from a 'Sara.' 'Please

call Sara,' maybe two or three a week,'' he said as he searched through the stack.

''Here's another one from Richards' Body Shop, 'your car is ready','' he read the message and put it and one of Sara's messages in his coat pocket.

''I'm going to go through his files,'' he said, pointing to two wooden file cabinets positioned on either side of the credenza.

''You see if there's something on that thing,'' he said, pointing to a computer on his credenza.

''I'm not going to search through his hard drive. Besides, I'm sure it's password protected,'' I said.

''Quit being a pansy and just check it,'' he said.

Reluctantly, I turned on the computer and sure enough it asked me for a password.

''See, it wants a password,'' I said.

''Go ask Max for one,'' Smitty said without looking up from the files he was searching through.

''Are you crazy? There's not a law firm in the world that's going to let a reporter rifle through their computer network. She'd throw us out right now if she knew you were going through those files,'' I said.

''Okay, here we go. Waste Solutions Inc.,'' he said as he removed a thin manila folder from the file cabinet and opened it on the desk.

It was easy to read the disappointment on Smitty's face when the file turned out to be nothing but a collection of news stories about the project and some preliminary legal research.

''I was hoping this would be something,'' he said, more to himself than me.

"Maybe it's nothing, because there is nothing. You better keep your mind open to the idea that this is probably just a big coincidence," I said.

"Right, Sammy. Right."

SIX

AFTER LEAVING Jeff's office, Smitty and I stopped at a nearby deli for lunch. We ordered and found a table near the window. Smitty used my mobile phone to call the number for Sara.

"Hello, is Sara in?" he asked and then said to me, "Must be her work number."

"Hello Sara, my name is Wayne Smith, I'm a reporter for the *Capitol Times* in Wasatch City, Utah. I'm in town working on a story about Jeff Leapingdeer," he said.

There was a pause while she responded.

"Yes that's right, in Wasatch City. I was wondering if my associate and I could stop by and talk to you about Jeff this afternoon?" Smitty said, followed by a brief pause. Then Smitty started writing an address on a deli napkin.

"That's great," he said, "we'll see you in an hour."

"Seems nice," he said as he hung up the phone.

I started to protest going with him to the meeting but decided against it. My flight wasn't for several more hours and although I would never admit it to

Smitty, I was finding his investigation rather interesting even if it was one dead end after another.

"Was she curious about why you were writing a story about Jeff?" I said when he had finished making his notes on the napkin.

"A little surprised. But I'm sure she knows who his mother was and she probably thinks there's some sort of news angle there," he said as a waitress dropped our sandwiches in front of us. Smitty attacked his as though he thought it might run away.

"So what do you think? Getting a little suspicious yet?" he said through a mouth ninety percent full of a corned beef on rye.

"Well, I know more now, so I have a few more questions. But I don't know about suspicious. Still, just seems like an incredibly sad coincidence to me," I said.

"Could be. But there is one more angle to this story that I haven't let you in on yet," he said with a grin. This was Smitty style, only feeding you enough to keep you interested and when you start losing interest, tantalizing you with another little morsel.

"And that is?"

"Ralf Voss," he said with a smile worthy of someone who had just finished the *New York Times* daily crossword puzzle.

"State Senator Ralf Voss?" I asked, thoroughly confused, which is exactly the way Smitty wanted me.

"That's right. Died in a skiing accident seven weeks ago."

Until his death Ralf Voss had been the leading candidate to run against Governor Beckstead in the next election. Smitty, who detested Beckstead, simply loved Voss.

"And now you're going to tell me he was murdered as well?" I said.

"Now there are three 'accidents'," he said, using his fingers to indicate quotation marks around the word "accidents."

"Okay Smitty, this is where we part company. Voss had no connection to the Leapingdeers," I said.

"Now hold on. 'Bout three weeks before he died, Voss called the Office of Legislative Research and General Council and opened a protected bill file. He was planning to run a bill on the dump."

A bill file is what a state legislator opens when he wants the Office of Legislative Research and General Council to begin drafting a bill for him to sponsor in the next legislative session. A protected file is supposed to remain confidential between that office and the legislator until the legislator is ready to go public with it. I was a little surprised that Smitty knew about the file, but did not want to give him the satisfaction of asking him how he learned about it.

"Three weeks later, he's dead," Smitty concluded.

"I hate to break this to you Smitty, because I know Voss was your boy, but there are a lot of legislators with bills opposing that dump and none of them have had any 'accidents'," I said, mimicking his quotations.

"Look, I know Baby Grand and Voss hated each

other, but you're going to have to admit that Voss was no lightweight. He wouldn't run some bill just for the sake of running it. If he was running a bill it was because he knew something or had some idea—something real, something substantial,'' he said, though it was hard to hear now that the other half of his sandwich was wedged into his mouth.

I didn't want to, but I had to admit that Smitty was right. Voss wouldn't run a meaningless bill. If he was going to run it, it was real.

''What did the police report say about his death?'' I asked.

''Get this, there isn't one.'' He had it down to about a fourth of a sandwich by now.

''What?''

He held up his hand asking me to wait until he swallowed.

''When these ski resorts have accidents, even fatal ones, they just call the paramedics, not the police. I talked to the ones that pulled him out of the woods that morning. They said he made a wrong turn going too fast. Whack. Right into a quakie,'' he said, slamming his hands together to emphasize the ''whack.''

''Could have been pushed,'' he added.

''That's what the paramedics said?'' I asked.

''Well, no but they couldn't rule it out either,'' I said.

''And of course not. They're not trained investigators either,'' I said.

''No they're not. And if this were a single incident I wouldn't even bat an eye at it. But when you consider it in light of the other two, then..." He looked at me as if to say, "Don't you get it, Sammy?"

I needed to get away from Smitty. His conspiracy theory was beginning to make a little too much sense to me. But I wasn't about to admit it to him, not right now anyway.

Sara—we still did not know her last name—was a junior partner in a law firm not far from Jeff's office. Her office was much smaller than Jeff's and austere in comparison. However, she was all the decoration her office needed. Medium height, slender build, deep blue eyes, and a gregarious smile of the kind not often found on an attorney.

"It's a pleasure to meet you," she said after we had introduced ourselves.

"The pleasure is all ours, Ms...." I said, taking one of two seats in front of her desk. Smitty grunted his way into the other.

"Newman, Sara Newman. But please, call me Sara," she said.

"Thank you," I said. "I was sorry to here about Jeff's accident."

"It's been very hard. Coming on the heels of his mother's death the way it did," she said.

"Did you know Ms. Leapingdeer?" Smitty asked.

"We had met on a couple of occasions. But I couldn't really say I knew her, no," she said.

"I never had the pleasure of meeting her," I said, "but people that knew her said she was a very sweet lady."

"Yes, she was," she said then turned her attention to Smitty. "Tell me about your story, Mr. Smith."

"Please, everybody calls me Smitty. I had hoped to kind of ease into this but since you have asked," he took a deep breath, "I'm looking into the chance that Jeff's death was not accidental."

Instinctively, she brought her hand to her mouth and tears welled up in her eyes. "Oh my..."

"I realize that this is a hard time for you, Ms. Newman. I'm sorry for intruding—"

"That's not it, Mr. Smith. I'm not comfortable with the police account of what happened either," she said through her tears. "Frankly, I've tried to accept that what they say happened, but I can't."

"What do you mean?" Smitty asked, sitting up on the edge of his seat.

"Jeff and I have known...well, knew each other for seven years. And yes, he did occasionally drink, but only in small amounts. I never in our seven-year relationship saw him drunk. The only time he ever drank was socially when others did and then he would nurse the same drink all night. And he never, never drove drunk. Never."

"The police say that there was some alcohol in his blood when...it happened," Smitty said, searching for the right word.

"I know, I know that's what made me so sick about the police report. It was because of me that he had anything at all to drink that night," she said as a fresh wave of tears rolled down her checks. "We met for dinner the day he returned from his mother's funeral.

He was very shaken up by the whole thing. You can imagine. He complained about not being able to sleep since it happened. He looked awful. I practically forced him to have a scotch with his dinner. Thinking it would help relax him, make him sleep better. He drank most of the scotch—mainly because I insisted—but hardly touched his dinner," she said.

"So he was drinking that night," I said.

"Yes. One drink. One," she said as she held up her index finger. "I assure you he was very sober when he left the restaurant."

"Where was he going after dinner?" Smitty said.

"He said he was meeting some people at a place called Mountain Home Inn."

"Mountain Home Inn?"

"Yes, it's a small hotel and restaurant about two thirds of the way up Mt. Tamalpais."

"Is it on a..." Smitty was turning back pages in his notebook, "Panoramic Highway?"

"That's right, the road he was killed on."

"Did he say what the meeting was about?"

"No, he wasn't very talkative that night. Every time I brought it up, he changed the subject," she said as if she could still see him sitting in front of her. "But he said he had to do it himself."

"And that was the last time you spoke with him?"

She nodded yes, unable to answer audibly.

"What were Jeff's living arrangements?" Smitty asked.

"He lived in an apartment downtown."

"Is it still...I mean has his stuff been...moved?"

Smitty said, not quite sure how to ask if Jeff's apartment was still intact.

"Yes it is. I don't really know what to do about it. With his mother dead, and his only brother in prison in New Mexico, I guess I'm the only one available. But I just haven't been able to face it. I mean what am I going to do with all his stuff? I just don't know," she said. Her eyes momentarily glazed over as if she were talking to herself.

"Do you know if it would be possible for us to take a look around his place?" Smitty said, bringing her back to the conversation.

"I have a key. If you think it would help you are welcome to take it," she said and began removing a key from a ring that had been sitting on her desk. She handed it to Smitty.

"The address?" Smitty said.

"Let me jot it down for you," she said and wrote the address on a Post-it note, also handing it to Smitty.

I could tell Smitty had other questions he wanted to ask, but even he could see Sara had had enough. He closed his notepad and put it in his pocket.

"I'm sorry to put you through this, Ms. Newman. Thank you for your time," he said as he stood. I followed his lead.

"Mr. Smith, do you know who would have reason to do something like this to Jeff?" she said when we were almost out her office door.

"Not yet," he said. "Did he ever mention anything to you about a company called Waste Solutions Inc., or about a nuclear waste dump they were planning to put on the Pishute Indian Reservation in Utah?''

"Oh yes. We talked about it all the time. He was planning to sue them over it,'' she said.

"Really?''

"Yes. He was holding off doing anything publicly because of his mother. You are aware she supported the project?''

"Yes.''

"Well, Jeff wanted to make every effort to change her mind first before he did anything. Showing the proper respect for her was very important to him,'' she said.

"Did he have any contact with anyone at Waste Solutions?'' Smitty asked.

"Only once that I know of. A man by the name of Gray...Green...''

"Griggs?'' I said. Smitty shot a surprised glance my way.

"Yes, Griggs. That's it, Griggs. He called Jeff once about a month ago. I believe Jeff's mother had asked him to call,'' Sara said.

"Why did he call?'' Smitty asked.

"I think they thought they might be able to neutralize Jeff. But it didn't take Jeff long to disabuse them of the idea. I don't think the two ever spoke again. If so, Jeff never mentioned it to me,'' she said.

"Is it possible the two did talk again and just didn't mention it to you?'' Smitty asked.

"Oh yes, it's possible. He did keep things from me,

but he did go out of his way to keep me updated on all his projects,'' she said.

''And you think Mary had this Griggs fellow call Jeff,'' Smitty said.

''That's what Jeff said. Do you think these people had something to do with...'' There was a horrified look on her face as she let the sentence trail off.

''No, Ms. Newman. I don't know anything yet. I'm looking at everything I can. That's all.''

I was relieved to see Smitty show some discretion.

SEVEN

"WELL WHAT DO YOU think now?" Smitty asked as we walked from Sara's office building and out onto the street.

I almost responded with a quip, but realized that it had been a serious question. Smitty wanted my honest opinion.

"Nothing I heard in there hurt your theory that there is more to this than meets the eye. But a person's family and loved ones tend to see what they want to see. I hate to say it, Smitty, but Sara may just be in denial that Jeff would do something so stupid," I said.

"That is a possibility, I'll have to grant you that. But if they were dating or whatever, she would know what his drinking habits were," Smitty said as he hailed a cab.

"Yeah that's what gives her story credibility. But you shouldn't close your eyes to the fact that in times like these, when emotions are running high like hers, the human capacity for self-delusion is at its peak," I said.

As I finished my sentence a cab pulled to the curb and we both got in.

"I know, I know," Smitty said, shutting the door to the cab. As he turned to me I could see a look of melancholy I had never seen on him before.

"Where to?" asked the cabby.

From his pocket Smitty produced the address to Richards' Body Shop and handed it to the cabby.

"When I was sixteen, my father killed himself," Smitty said, looking straight ahead. He made a gun with fingers and put it to his temple to show how it had happened. "I was 20 years old before I could admit—even to myself—that it wasn't an accident. Even today I have a hard time calling it a suicide. But for the four years after it happened, I knew it was an accident. Not a single doubt. Anybody told me any different just didn't know what they were talking about.

"But then one day, it was the Friday after Thanksgiving, I was alone in my mother's house—she and my sisters were out shopping—and it just dawned on me. I remember being kind of startled by the thought," he said, still looking straight ahead. "It was an actual physical shock to my system," he said and bristled as if he suddenly felt chilled.

Smitty had on the rarest occasions mentioned only the most innocuous details of his personal life. Now suddenly, from nowhere, he drops this on me. I was not sure how to react. I caught myself staring at him as if he were a stranger.

"She could be doing the same thing, don't you think?" he said as if he hadn't noticed the awkwardness of the moment.

"Yes, that's...huh...right," I stuttered out.

"But on the other hand, it is one thing to say the man was rarely drunk and another thing to say he was never drunk," he said.

"And what Max said kind of backs up what Sara said. Max never saw him drunk either, much less drunk and behind the wheel," I said, unable to resist the urge to encourage Smitty.

"Tell me about this Griggs who called Jeff. How do you know him?" he asked.

I spent the rest of the ride to the body shop explaining to Smitty who Tom Griggs was and how I knew him.

RICHARDS' REPAIR and Body was a small shop with four stalls and an office in the middle. Three of the stalls were occupied by cars, each with a mechanic busy under the hood.

"May I help you?" said the thirtysomething mechanic as we approached. The patch on his shirt revealed him as Bobby.

"Yes thank you, I'm Wayne Smith, this is Sam McKall," Smitty said, shaking the man's hand and ignoring the grease. I was forced to do the same.

"Bobby Richards, what can I do for ya," he said.

"Nice to meet you, Mister Richards. I've got just a question or two about a car you repaired a few weeks back."

"Shoot," Bobby said putting his hands in his pockets.

"The owner was a guy named Leapingdeer, Jeff Leapingdeer. He—"

"Police have already been in here about that," he said, a little puzzled.

"Yes I know, we met with the police this morning and—"

"Who are you guys?" he asked, shoving his hands deep into his pants pockets.

"I'm a reporter for a newspaper in Utah. I've only got a couple of questions, Mister Richards," Smitty said.

I could see on his face that Bobby was more than a little nervous to be talking to us.

"I already told the police everything I know. That car was in good working order when it left here," he said, removing his right hand from his pocket long enough to point to the ground for emphasis.

"I have no doubt that it was. We just want to know if you could tell us what caused the accident?" Smitty said.

"Brakes failed," he said.

"How?" Smitty said.

"One of the hoses coming out of the master cylinder ruptured," he said feeling a little more comfortable.

"Was it cut or punctured in some way?" Smitty said.

"Fatigue," he said as though it were the most obvious thing in the world.

"Fatigue?" Smitty said.

"Just old and cracked. That's it."

"If I told you someone had been trying to kill Mr.

Leapingdeer would that change the way you looked at it?'' Smitty said.

''I seen all kinds of problems with all kind of hoses and that thing was just fatigued. May have been faulty when they installed it at the factory,'' he said. I could tell he was digging into his position and that any further questioning was futile.

But Smitty pressed on.

''How often do you see that kind of thing? Fatigued hoses?'' he said, almost mocking the man.

''Time to time.''

''Once a week? Once a month? Once a year?'' Smitty said, doing his best to draw anything out of the man he could.

''Less than once a week, more than once a year,'' he said, smiling to let Smitty know that he wasn't quite as dumb he thought.

''Bottom line is you'd seen it before and didn't see anything out of the ordinary,'' Smitty summed up.

''That's the bottom line,'' he said.

''I think I got that,'' said Smitty, making notes in his notebook.

''Look, I'm sorry this Leapingdeer got drunk and killed himself, but I know his brakes were working just fine when he had the accident. That's what the police told me anyway,'' he said genuinely confused as to why his work on the car was being questioned for a second time.

''Yes, the police told us the same thing this morning,'' Smitty said.

''Then what's the problem?'' he asked.

"Mister Richards, I'm sorry if I've given you the wrong impression here. I don't think you did anything wrong at all. But I do believe that someone may have been trying to kill Mr. Leapingdeer and I'm looking into the possibility that they may have done it by tampering with his car in some way," Smitty said.

"I don't know about all that. All I know is he had an old, cracked brake hose that ruptured and caused his brakes not to work a few weeks ago. He brought the car in here and I fixed it as good as new. What happened to the car once it left here I can't say."

"THAT SEEMED pretty clear cut," I said to Smitty in the back of yet another dirty cab.

"What? That guy?" he said, jerking his thumb over his shoulder in the direction of the garage.

"Yeah, a simple worn-out rubber hose, that's all," I said.

"You saw as well as I did, that guy wasn't really thinking about his answers. He was just saying what he thought was right. He wasn't that sure of himself. I bet the guy doesn't even remember taking the old hose off," Smitty said.

"Even if that's true—and I'm not saying it is—there's still no evidence that the car was tampered with."

"That's true. But I'm not a prosecuting attorney taking a case to trial," he said.

"Still, you have some standard of fact or evidence that needs to be met before you just assume the car was tampered with," I said, a little incredulous.

"Give me a break, Sammy. So that was a dead end and I'll probably never be able to prove that Leapingdeer's car was tampered with. But nothing I heard from Bobby back there is going to make me foreclose on the idea either. The car comes in and the hose had some cracks in it. So what? Did he really examine it that closely? In his heart of hearts is he really so sure those cracks caused the rupture? Or did he just assume that the cracks caused the leaks, throw the old hose away and install a new one?" he said.

"I don't know," I said.

"Neither do I. But assume with me for a minute that he didn't really look at the hose when he took it off. Just took it off and threw it away. Probably done it a thousand times. Then the police show up, it's clear they think Leapingdeer killed himself in a DUI and they're just trying to wrap up a loose end. What's Bobby going to say when they ask him about that hose? He's going to tell them what they want to hear. It's the best thing for him and the police. Clean and simple. After that, anybody who asks about it is going to get the same answer. I doubt that guy really knows what the truth even is."

"That's a pretty convenient stretch, Smitty. There's still the chance that he did, in fact, check the hose," I said, suddenly aware that Smitty and I seemed to keep having the same conversation over and over.

"Two things you learn as a reporter, Sam." He held up one finger. "People lie more often than you think and"—he held up a second finger—"people have bad and selective memories, so even when they're not lying, what they tell you may not, in fact, be true."

"You're the reporter," I said, shrugging my shoulders.

"I think we have established that," he said.

THE CAB DROPPED us off in front of a high-rise condominium building in downtown San Francisco. It was actually a relief to find that the building had a security officer who was insisting that only residents or their invited guests be allowed in the building. My relief was soon replaced by shock when Smitty talked his way into the building and waved me past security and over to the elevators.

"How'd you do that?" I said after the doors had closed.

"If I told you, you wouldn't respect me in the morning," Smitty said with a wry grin.

The elevator stopped on the sixteenth floor where we found apartment number 1631. Using the key that Sara had given us, Smitty unlocked the door and we walked in.

It was a two-bedroom apartment, with a kitchen, living room, and a beautiful view of the city. The bed was unmade and a couple of dishes were left in the sink but other than that, the apartment closely resembled his office, neat and moderately decorated. There were two pictures on a small coffee table in the living room. One was of Jeff and Sara and appeared to have been taken of them while seated at a restaurant table somewhere. The second was of Jeff, his mother, and another man walking on a beach. All three were smiling, almost laughing.

"Who's this in the picture with Mary and Jeff?" I said to Smitty, who was snooping around a desk on the other side of the room.

"Probably Jeff's brother Calvin. He's in prison down around Albuquerque," Smitty said after glancing over his shoulder.

"Why is it always the good son?" I asked more to myself than anyone else.

"It's not, it's just more poignant when it is," Smitty offered.

I walked over to the desk just as Smitty opened one of its drawers. Among other contents, there were a dozen or so microtapes and a microrecorder. Each of the labels on the tapes were well worn, as if they had been erased and reused many times. On each label there was written a date.

Smitty randomly picked one of the tapes and popped it in the recorder. After several moments of hissing Jeff's voice came on:

"Today is Monday, June 14. Change lunch appointment with Bruce to Thursday. Set up meeting with the Harrison's. Finalize Mason versus West-Chem brief for tomorrow's filling..."

Smitty turned the recorder off and started putting the remainder of the tapes in his pockets.

"You're not going to take those, are you?" I said, suddenly feeling like I was party to a breaking-and-entering.

"No, of course not," Smitty said as he kept shoving the tapes into his pocket.

I just stared at him for a second.

"What? Whose permission should I get?"

"I don't know, but I don't think you should just come in here and take things," I said.

"If it will make you feel any better I'll tell Sara I got them and return them to her when I'm done listening to them," he said as he slid the last tape into his pocket. I thought about it for a second and that did seem okay.

Leaving the desk, I walked into the bedroom. It was furnished with a king-size bed, chest of drawers and an upholstered chair over which was laid a pair of suit paints. In the closet I found ten or so suits; a few sport coats and slacks; some casual clothes; and a small collection of Sara's things.

"Looks like he just bought a new recorder," Smitty said from the kitchen area. I walked in and found him looking at a box for a brand-new microrecorder which he had just taken out of the trash.

"That must have been what he used to keep himself organized," I said.

"Must have been," Smitty said putting the box back into the garbage.

We looked around Jeff's apartment for another fifteen minutes or so but found nothing out of the ordinary. We left having pilfered nothing but the tapes.

EIGHT

ON THE PLANE BACK to Wasatch I thought of everything that had happened in the last ten hours. Was it simply a collection of random events and facts that only stood out because we spent so much time and effort hunting them? Were we latching onto any little sliver of information that provided a link, no matter how tenuous? Or was it more like one of those computer-generated optical illusions that at first glance, looks like a picture of TV static, but when viewed in the right way a sophisticated 3-D picture comes into focus?

I tried to make sense of the whole thing until I could no longer concentrate on it. As the details of Smitty's investigation faded into the background, my thoughts turned to Tracey.

I had not heard from her since the day she called and invited me to her family's weekend retreat. A few days after our conversation, a plane ticket arrived via FedEx at my office. No note or explanation. Just a plane ticket. I had waited for a call, but none came. This was the frustrating thing about Tracey.

It was a long flight, giving me a lot of time to think, and I had to admit that a lot of what had happened—

or in this case not happened—was my fault. Tracey and I were living nearly 2,000 miles apart so every time it became even the slightest bit awkward to take the next step in the relationship I shied away, telling myself that with the distance between us the timing was just not right.

What frustrated me the most about the situation was that this indecisiveness was foreign to both of our personalities yet at the moment of truth, when we stared each other in the eyes, quietly and simultaneously we both laid our cards face down and folded.

That, I decided, would not be the case on my trip. York Beach, Maine, would provide either a final resting place for my hopes of a relationship with Tracey or the catalyst for the relationship I had wanted all along. Whatever the case, I promised myself that I was not going to leave there unsure of what our future might be.

I called Tracey to let her know that I had received the ticket and left a message on her voice mail.

I WOKE THE FOLLOWING morning thinking about Ralf Voss. There was at least one thing Smitty had said the day before that was absolutely true: Voss was no lightweight. If he had been planning to run a bill on the nuke dump he had probably come up with a legitimate idea that he thought would stop the Consortium. Given the political rivalry between Voss and Governor Beckstead, I was sure he planned on using the bill as a platform to show that Beckstead was ineffective as Governor. But putting political differences aside, it could be said that on this one, at least, we were on the same side. That being the case, I rationalized, there was no reason why Senator Voss's idea should die with him. So I decided to make an attempt to find out what he had been up to.

My guess was that Voss had been working with Valerie Turpin in the Office of Legislative Council and Research as the Analyst on his bill. During my time in the Governor's office I had struck up a friendship with Valerie.

Valerie had recently been the victim of a stalker who had been phoning her at home with threatening messages and even going as far as breaking into her office and spray-painting obscenities on the wall. It had created quite a stir at the Capitol.

I felt guilty about not having called to check on her before, only doing so now that I needed a favor from her. I thought about not calling at all but decided that would be worse than calling now that I had a favor to ask.

I called her when I arrived in my office and she politely accepted an invitation to lunch later that day.

My next order of business was calling Tracey. I dialed the number and she answered on the second ring.

"Hello Tracey, Sam."

"Hi Sam. Where have you been?"

"I was in Sacramento for the NGA meeting and then up to San Francisco for a day doing a little favor for Smitty."

"Smitty's asking you for favors now," she said.

"Yeah, he's working on a story about Jeff Leapingdeer, Mary's son. He died in an auto accident a couple weeks ago. San Francisco PD was jerking him around a bit so I helped smooth the way for him," I said.

"I wish Smitty would ask me for a favor," she said, then changed the subject. "I'm sorry we haven't spoken sooner, but I have been trying to call."

"I haven't gotten any messages from you."

"You're not the only one who doesn't like to leave voice mails," she said.

"I'm just calling to see what the plan is for this weekend," I said.

"Good, that was why I was trying to call you, too. I really appreciate you doing this for me. It is very sweet."

"That's my M.O.," I said.

"The whole thing is really casual. My parents have a summer home in between Kennebunkport and Portsmouth in a little place called York Beach."

"I've heard of it. Sounds nice."

"I think you'll enjoy it. Anyway, it'll be real casual, boating, swimming, sailing. Three days, two nights and you're done," she said.

"Bathing suits and casual clothes then?"

"That's all you'll need. I'll pick you up at the airport in Portland," she said.

"Just your family, right?" I said trying to draw her out on why I was invited.

"Yeah, all my married sisters, their husbands and kids," she said through a melodramatic sigh.

"And me," I added.

"And you," she said.

I could tell there was more she wanted to say, so I waited for further explanation but none came.

Just then Governor Beckstead came into my office and had a seat in one of the chairs in front of my desk.

"Well I've got to go, I'll see you at the airport," I said to Tracey to wrap up the conversation.

"Looking forward to it. I'll explain more when I see you at the airport. Good-bye," she said with a tinge of relief in her voice and hung up the phone.

"Going out of town?" the Governor said after I had hung up the phone.

"Yeah, going to visit a friend over Labor Day weekend," I said.

"Good. Did you get your other friend taken care of yesterday?" He was asking about Smitty and letting me know that he was not entirely comfortable with me helping him out.

"I did. And you'll be happy to know that he's chasing down one red herring after another," I said.

"What is it you two are working on?" he asked.

His question put me in a real delicate situation. I owed him an honest answer, but I knew if I gave him one he would use it to poison my relationship with Smitty. The next time he and Smitty talked he would just mention that he knew what Smitty was investigating and that would make Smitty wonder how much of what he thought actually stayed between him and me. I decided to take the less-is-more approach.

"He's doing a story on Mary and Jeff Leapingdeer," I said.

"He needed your help on that?"

"The San Francisco Police Department was jerking him around on some of the details on Jeff's accident so I called Penny McGriff to help open some doors for him and it turned out they would only give the information to me, not to him. They just refused to deal with him," I explained, thinking that he would enjoy the thought of Smitty being snubbed.

"I wish we could do the same thing," he said.

"Same thing?" I said.

"Refuse to work with Smitty," he said, less than half joking.

"Well we can't, and that's why I do my best to be on his good side," I said, reinforcing what I had told him a thousand times. Intellectually he knew I was right, but emotionally he just wanted everybody to hate Smitty as much as he did and it bothered him that I wouldn't.

"Anyway, I got one of those nuke guys coming in here this afternoon. Guy by the name of Tom Griggs, supposed to be the project coordinator or something. Wants to tell us how we don't have anything to worry about. He'll be here at 2:00; I want you to be in the meeting. Can you?" He said getting up from his chair.

"That's no problem, I'll look forward to it. How long's this been on the schedule?" I said.

"This Griggs guy called while you were in D.C.

for the NRC hearing. See you then," he said as he left my office.

I spent the rest of the morning clearing my desk of problems that had piled up while I had been gone, and returning a long list of phone calls.

Finally at about 11:45 I headed down to Market Street to a restaurant, appropriately named The Market Street Grill, where Valerie and I had planned to meet. I got a table and was waiting for her at the appointed time.

NINE

WASATCH CITY IS not known as a "restaurant town" but the Market Street Grill is one of a few diamonds in the rough. With fresh seafood flown in from each coast daily, it is nearly impossible to find better seafood anywhere and absolutely impossible to find one among those that are similarly landlocked.

Valerie arrived ten or so minutes late. I was shocked when I saw her, thinking she must have put on ten years in the few weeks it had been since I had seen her last. Her eyes were cold and distant, and deep lines had formed around her mouth and cheeks. I stood to greet her as she approached the table.

"Thanks for coming, Valerie. How are you doing?" I said. She could tell by the look on my face that I didn't think she was doing so well.

"I'm doing better than I look," she said. I hoped that the look on my face hadn't given my thoughts away.

"You look great," I lied. "I've just been worried about you."

As she was taking her seat I said, "Can I ask what has been going on or would you rather not talk about it?" I was unsure if that was the right thing to say.

"Oh, I don't mind talking about it, it's the living through it that really bothers me," she said and momentarily her face brightened with a smile which disappeared as she continued.

"About six weeks ago I got a letter at home. It started off by saying he had been watching me and how much he liked me and wanted to meet me. Seemed harmless, but something about the way it was written…I don't know, made me nervous. But there were no threats, so I ignored it.

"Then two days later I get a call. 'Don't ignore me Valerie, I get mad when I am ignored.'" And then click. Just hung up. But it wasn't a person's voice. It was a computer. You know, like someone had programmed a computer to say it. It scared me witless. I freaked out. I called the police and reported the whole thing. They came over and patted me on the back and told me everything was going to be fine. But by then I had thrown the letter away. I kind of got the feeling that they either didn't believe me or thought that I was blowing it way out of proportion. After they left I decided to spend the night in a hotel.

"When I got to work the next morning there was a note that had come over the fax. It said, 'You have another chance today, don't ignore me. It makes me very angry'," she said.

"Where was it faxed from?" I asked.

"The Kinko's on 2nd South and State," she said and was about to continue when the waitress came by to get our order. Even though I had completely lost my appetite I ordered the blackened salmon so that she would feel comfortable ordering, but she just asked for the salad and chowder. That sounded good to me too, so I changed my order.

"I called the police again. Sent the office into a panic. That night another call. There have been so many now I can't remember them all. But by then the police had my phone tapped. It went on like that for another few weeks. Phone calls at home. Threatening letters. Then one morning, the morning of Senator Voss's funeral I got in late. Everyone did, we all went to the funeral. My office had been broken into and there was a spray-painted message on the walls: 'don't ignore me,' it said, among other more disgusting things. Nothing missing from the office but my gym bag with dirty workout clothes in it. I snapped, just broke down. I had to leave town. I went up and stayed with an old college roommate of mine in the San Juan Islands in Washington State.

"The police had no luck tracking the guy down, but the calls and letters stopped. So a little more than two weeks ago I decided it was time to come back. At first nothing, no calls, no messages, no letters, no faxes. Nothing. I began to feel a little better about things.

"But just over a week ago, I got another one, same computer voice: 'I enjoyed our trip, you should wear the black bikini more.' You can't imagine the sick feeling. Cannot imagine," she said.

"What'd you do?" I said, feeling pretty sick nonetheless.

"That's the frustrating thing. There's nothing to do.

I can't hide. He knows what I'm doing when I do it. Even when I leave town. There's no escape."

"It must be...be...awful," I said, unable to come up with a strong enough word.

"That was the last one, at least for now anyway. It's ruined my life. I can't eat, sleep, work. I shower with the curtain open. I got an alarm system installed. My friends and co-workers are afraid to be with me. It's just horrible.

"You want to know what my worst fear is?" she asked.

"What?" I said, even though I was not sure I really wanted to know.

"That this is the end of it. That this guy just goes away and never gets caught. I can't imagine a worry-free second in my life as long as I know he's roaming the streets."

Her story turned out to be much worse than I had expected and I began to feel embarrassed about my real reason for inviting her to lunch.

Thankfully our salads arrived.

"Valerie, I'm really sorry you're having to go through this. If there is anything I can do, or the Governor's office can do, please let me know." Obviously there was little or nothing that the Governor's office could do to help, but it sounded good and I was sincere.

"I'm sure you didn't invite me down here to hear about my horror story life," she said after barely touching her salad. At that point, I had no intention of bothering her with my little request.

"It's nothing. I've already taken care of it. Don't worry about it," I said as casually as I could.

"Please don't do this, Sam. Everyone is trying to be so nice. My entire workload has practically been reassigned, no one wants to trouble me. But believe me it will be nice to worry about something else for a change," she said.

I looked at her for a moment and considered what I should do. I decided a few questions wouldn't hurt. It might, for a second at least, take her mind off things.

"If you're sure," I said, pushing my salad away to signify that I was ready to do business.

"Absolutely," she said with a nod of her head.

"Okay. I understand that some time before his accident, Ralf Voss opened a bill file on the west desert nuke dump," I said. The surprise was evident on her face.

"How did you know that?" she asked.

"I'll tell you, but it has to stay between you and me," I said.

"Alright."

"Wayne Smith told me."

"How did he find out?"

"I have no idea, and he's not about to tell me either. Who knows, Voss could have told him. He and Smitty were close."

She didn't say anything for a moment while she considered what to do.

"We're off the record, right?" she finally said.

"Yes."

"He did open a file."

"What was his plan?"

"That I don't know. But I'll tell you this, he thought he had something," she said.

"What do you mean?"

"When he called to open the file, I told him we had at least 25 files open on the dump. They were clogging up the system, so I thought I'd try to talk him out of opening his. But he said, 'Don't worry Val, I'm not wasting your time. You'll see. Open the file but don't do anything. I'm going to send you some information. After you get it, we'll get together and I'll explain everything'," she said.

"When was this?"

"About two months ago," she said.

"Did he ever send you anything?"

Here she paused again before answering.

"About ten days after the call, I got a FedEx from a Boston address. It was a stack of papers—20 or 30 sheets. And a note from him."

"What did the note say?" I said. Clearly I was getting into an area where she was not comfortable. But some of the life had returned to her eyes so I decided to keep asking questions until she didn't want to answer anymore.

"It just said, 'This is the info we talked about. I'll explain when I get back to town.' Before you ask let me say, yes I looked through it. Glanced at it is more like it. It's a lot of numbers and terminology that I didn't understand, so I just put it in the file and waited on him to call," she said.

There was a brief interruption while our clam chowder was served. She took a few token sips. I did likewise.

"Did he ever call?" I said after she had lost interest in her chowder.

"Yes, we were supposed to meet on the day after his accident." Wouldn't Smitty love to be hearing this?

"What would I need to do to get a look at the stuff he sent you?" I asked.

"I don't really know. I don't think it has ever been an issue, at least as long as I've been there," she said.

"Who should I talk to about it?" I said.

"Why don't you let me find out; it'll give me something to do. I'll call you later this afternoon."

AT 2:00 THAT AFTERNOON I was sitting with the Governor across a small conference table from Tom Griggs, Project Coordinator for Waste Solutions.

The people Governor Beckstead likes or who he wants to impress, he meets with in the ceremonial office. Close friends and associates, or people he wants to make feel like insiders, are met in the private office, behind the ceremonial office. But if the Governor doesn't like you, or you are in his doghouse for some reason, your meeting with the Governor is in a small conference room as far away from the governor's office as you can get and still be in our offices.

The staff didn't even need to ask. They took Tom Griggs immediately to the small conference room.

"Governor, I just wanted to come by and assure

you that we are interested in your input on how this project is done. We are taking every possible step to assure that it will be safe and clean. At no time will it endanger the health or safety of any Utahn. And finally we wanted to assure you that this will only be a temporary facility. As soon as the federal government fulfills its statutory obligation to provide a permanent site for this waste, it will all be moved, and our facility closed," Griggs said. His last statement brought a contemptuous laugh from the Governor which in turn made me laugh.

"Griggs, let's just make a deal right now, you and me. I won't treat you like a stone-cold idiot and you don't treat me like one either," the Governor said, leaning forward on his elbows and looking Griggs in the eye.

"I'm sorry Governor, have I said something to offend you?" Griggs said leaning back and straightening his $150 tie.

"I don't know how many people believe that if by some miracle you are able to get this dump built that it will actually be temporary, but I'm not one of them. Once it's here, it's here for good."

"You don't understand. The federal—"

"You and I both know the federal government can do anything it damn well pleases. Once your project is built and the pressure is off them to finish Yucca Mountain, that project will be so dead, St. Peter himself won't be able to breathe life into it."

"I don't agree Governor—"

"Then I retract my promise, Mr. Griggs, because

you are an idiot. And I don't usually waste much time with idiots. So if you'll excuse me," the Governor said and got up to leave.

"Wait, Governor, can't we just talk about this?" Griggs said.

"What do we have to talk about? If you came here for my input, my input is go build your dump in somebody else's state, preferably a state that has actually produced some nuclear waste."

"I had hoped we could have a civil conversation about how this project can benefit your state. Financially," Griggs said as a last-ditch effort to keep the Governor in the room.

But the Governor was all the way out the door when he stopped and turned around.

"Mr. Griggs, I don't want your waste and I don't want your money. And you can expect me to be in your face every inch of the way. Every inch," he said and left.

I would have suggested another way, but that was certainly one way to handle Mr. Griggs.

I WORKED UNTIL lunch on Friday, then left to catch the plane to Maine. And frankly, I was so busy getting everything ready to go that I didn't even realize that Valerie had never called me back like she said she would. But even if it had occurred to me at the time, I would have thought nothing of it considering everything she was going through.

TEN

TRACEY WAS WAITING at the airport along with her mother and father when I landed. Her hair hung down to her shoulders. She was wearing a sleeveless summer dress and she practically ran into my arms as I walked off the jetway, giving me a long tight hug. It was the most intimate contact we had ever had.

"My parents are here; it wouldn't be a bad thing if they thought we were dating," she whispered into my ear as we were hugging. Then she released the hug and grabbed my hand.

"Mom, Dad, this is Sam. Sam, these are my parents," she said as she squeezed my arm and hand. I dropped my carry-on bag and extended my hand to shake her father's.

"It's very nice to meet you, Tracey's told me so many wonderful things about you, Mister and Mrs. Harmon," I lied. It was nice to meet them, but Tracey had hardly even mentioned them to me.

"Mike and Joan, please," he said, indicating that I should call them by their first names. "Tracey has barely stopped talking about you since she arrived yesterday."

"I can hardly believe that," I said and it was the

dead-on truth. I stole a glance at Tracey, whose grip had tightened considerably on my arm, and for the first time in my life I saw her blush.

"Anyway, it's nice that you could join us, Sam," her mother said and offered me a hug. I almost expected a whisper from her as well.

"Let's go get your bags," Tracey said.

"No need, I have everything right here," I said, reaching down to pick up my carry-on.

We walked out of the airport and Mike said, "Tracey, why don't you and Sam wait here and your mother and I will get the car."

Tracey waited until they were just barely out of earshot before saying, "I'm so sorry Sam. I thought I was going to come pick you up by myself and I could explain it all then. I guess I did too good of a sales job and my parents insisted on coming with me. Couldn't wait to meet you," she said.

"Why didn't you tell me when you invited me?" I said with a chuckle.

"Well, I sort of did. But I was afraid if I told you too much ahead of time you wouldn't come. But if I waited until you were here I knew you might not like it, but that you were too sweet to embarrass me in front of my family," she said and gratuitously batted her eyes at me.

"You hope I am," I said.

"Pleeease," she said.

"It's been so long since I was seeing anyone seriously that I'm not sure I remember how to act," I said.

"I'm sure it will all come back to you without much effort," she said.

"Let me ask you this," I said, trying to ride this thing as far as possible. "How serious are we?"

I noticed that out of the corner of her eye she spotted her parents turning the corner out of the parking garage. Without warning she reached one hand around the small of my back and pulled me to her. Her other hand was placed delicately on the back of my neck and before I really knew what was going on we were kissing. Not a long kiss, but a deep and passionate one, nonetheless.

"About that serious," she said and opened the door to her parents' Range Rover as it pulled to the curb.

THAT NIGHT Tracey and I were the center of attention. She had told the whole family about Senator Hansen's last campaign and the murder that almost cost us the election. I had been the campaign manager and she had been the communications director. She had brought copies of all of Smitty's stories where I had come off as much more of a hero than I really was. But I will have to admit that, at least in this case, it did not bother me too much.

Tracey sat by me the whole evening holding my hand, rubbing my back and without saying anything making a pretty good case that she was in love.

Of course there was only one unanswered question—how much of it was an act?

When we got to the end of our little tale of murder and politics it was well after midnight. Several of the brothers-in-law had already made their apologies and headed off to bed.

"Sam, I put some fresh sheets on your bed, and left some clean towels on the chest of drawers in your room," Tracey's mother said as she and Mark headed off to bed.

"I've enjoyed meeting you. Thanks for having me here this weekend," I said.

"We're glad to have you," Mark said.

As they left Tracey stood and offered me her hand. "Come on, I'll show you to your room," she said.

The Harmons' "cottage," as Tracey had called it, was nothing of the sort. It was a huge, airy place with lots of windows and drapes blowing in the trade winds. I followed Tracey down a long hallway past several bedrooms before getting to mine. She opened the door and turned on the light.

"Will this do?" she asked.

"This will more than do. It's nicer than my apartment," I said.

"I'm two doors down on the right if you need anything," she said and with a squeeze of my hand she was off to her room.

I WAS JUST dozing off to sleep when my bedroom door opened. The room was dark but I could tell by the slender silhouette that it was Tracey.

"Are you awake?" Her whisper was barely audible.

"Yes."

"I just wanted to say I'm sorry for putting you in

a position like this, but I really do appreciate it. You've been a good sport,'' she whispered as she leaned against the doorway.

''I'm enjoying it,'' I whispered.

''I just wanted to say thank you,'' she said and quietly closed my door.

THE NEXT MORNING I was awakened by the curtains being pulled open and sunlight flooding my room.

''Good morning,'' Tracey said, picking up a breakfast tray off the chest of drawers where she had set it momentarily.

''Good morning,'' I said, not sure how excited I was that Tracey was seeing me with pillow hair.

''I brought you some breakfast. I'm sorry we don't get the *Capitol Times* in York Beach,'' she said, knowing that I start every morning by reading the *Capitol Times*.

''I'll make do without it,'' I said. ''I had no idea you were so...domesticated.'' I was only half joking.

''You've never given me much of a chance,'' she said, placing the tray on my lap. She was dressed and ready for the day, in a floral print two-piece bathing suit and a sheer white sarong tied about her waist. It was a sight that could certainly get the blood pumping.

''We're going sailing in about 30 minutes. Can you be ready?''

''Easily,'' I said, trying not to be too obvious with my stare.

Tracey had never mentioned her prowess at sailing,

but watching her and her father as they navigated the southern Maine coast in the family Dehler 41, it was obvious that this was not her first regatta.

The weather, the boat, the day, Tracey, everything was beautiful. It was one of those rare days in life where design and circumstances align perfectly to create a day so amazing, so pristine, that living it seems miraculous and remembering it seems like a dream.

WE CAME OFF of the water about dusk. After a quick shower, we headed down to the Union Bluff Hotel, where I stuffed myself full of the best lobster I have ever eaten.

I was finding Tracey's family delightful. I had no sisters and my only brother died when I was only 9 years old, so I had very little experience in large families. But the Harmons had accepted me as one of the family from the very first moment I arrived in York Beach. I regretted that my stay with them would only last another 18 hours.

When the check came, I insisted on paying as my contribution to the weekend. Mike and Joan put up quite a battle but in the end Tracey solved it.

"Dad, just let Sam pay it. He can afford it, believe me," she said and gave me a wink across the table.

"That settles it," said Jerry, one of the brothers-in-law. "Sam pays."

I quickly produced a credit card and plopped it down on top of the check. After it was returned and I had signed the receipt Tracey suggested that we walk back to the "cottage."

"That's a good idea. I've got some things I need to talk to you about," I said so that only she could hear me.

"Sam and I are going to walk back. We'll see you a little later," she announced to the group.

"We'll see you at the cottage," her mother said.

We made our way down to Long Sands Beach, and began walking toward the Nubble Lighthouse, a beautiful old Victorian lighthouse built around 1876. Like the day had been, it was a perfect evening. We walked hand in hand without speaking for several minutes.

"Sam, thanks so much for being such a good sport," Tracey said, breaking the silence.

"I honestly can't tell you how much I have enjoyed it. I wish I didn't have to go tomorrow," I said.

"So do I, I wish we could both stay," she said, sliding her hand up my arm and pulling us closer together against the slight coolness of the evening trade winds.

"Why out of all the people you know, was I the one you invited here this weekend, Tracey?" I asked.

"That's easy, I can't fool my parents," she said, looking at the ground. But I could see a smile creep across her face.

Things fell quiet for a minute while the meaning of what she said settled over me.

"One of the reasons I resigned as Senator Hansen's Chief of Staff was the idea that there might...may be something between us," I said.

"I thought that's why you did it too, at first. But

then when you moved back to Wasatch City I decided I was probably wrong," she said.

"I guess I wasn't thinking that way. I didn't have a job, I was ready to leave Capitol Hill. Professionally, it was awkward just living somewhere without a job," I said, realizing for the first time that I too had been sending mixed signals.

"From time to time, you'd call or come back on business and we'd have dinner. I'd get my hopes up, but..." she let her sentence trail off into the night.

"I can't tell you how many times over the last year that I have had those same thoughts." As I spoke, she gently shook her head so that the breeze would blow her hair out of her eyes.

"Really?" She seemed genuinely surprised.

"Really. Let's not let that be the case anymore," I said.

"Let's not," she said.

Without saying another word, I stopped and pulled her to me. The moon was full and bright. I hesitated for just a moment and looked into her eyes. They were clear and beautiful and stared back into mine.

Our lips touched. Just barely at first. Then gradually it escalated.

I was vaguely aware of the waves lapping against our ankles, but at that moment nothing else, nothing at all, mattered.

IT WAS AFTER midnight when we arrived at the beach house. Tracey left me on the porch and went inside for a blanket. We laid in a two-person hammock talking until we fell asleep.

When I awoke the next morning the world was just as I had left it the night before, only completely new. Everything was the same, nothing was the same. The sun had risen on the southern Maine Coast and I knew. I knew. I couldn't believe it but I knew.

TRACEY HAD GOTTEN UP sometime after dawn and gone in to get ready for the day. I followed her a few minutes later. We were the first ones up and ready so we decided to make breakfast for everyone.

"So how are we going to handle this?" I asked as I began assembling the ingredients for the pancakes.

"You make the pancakes, I do the eggs and hashbrowns," she said, knowing full well that I wasn't talking about breakfast.

"You're very clever," I said, cracking eggs and pouring milk.

"Well you can't quit your job, I can't quit mine," she said.

"So it will have to be a long-distance relationship," I said in a half-question, half-statement fashion.

"I don't see how it can be any other way, at least right now. Do you?" she said, cracking the rest of the eggs into a heated frying pan.

"No, I don't."

"We can make it work. We both travel back and forth between Washington and Wasatch City on business. Between that and frequent flyer miles we can see each other two or three times a month, I bet,'' she said.

''That doesn't sound like that much to me,'' I said, pouring the first eight pancakes on the griddle.

''At least what little time we do have won't be wasted anymore,'' she said and gave me a playful pat in the rear.

''We'll just have to make it work.''

''We will.''

AFTER WE HAD served everyone breakfast, we headed out sailing and swimming. Tracey and I spent most of the morning lying on the beach, alternately napping and talking. All too quickly it was 3:00 and time for me to go. I packed my things and thanked the Harmons for a wonderful weekend. Then Tracey and I left for the airport in Portland.

''I can't come this week or the next, but I'll be in D.C. the following weekend,'' I said.

''I'll see if I can wait until then,'' she said and threw her arms around me.

We kissed good-bye and I boarded the plane.

HAD I KNOWN what awaited me in Wasatch City I might have never left Maine.

ELEVEN

WHEN I GOT BACK to my apartment in Wasatch City just after 11:00 p.m., I was both tired and exhilarated from my trip. After dumping my bag in the bedroom and throwing some leftover ham fried rice in the microwave, I checked my messages. There were several urgent-sounding messages from Bill Nelson, the Governor's Head of Security, asking me to return his call. The last one was more urgent.

"Sam, this is Bill again. I guess you are out of town. I hope so anyway. I've been trying to get in touch with you all weekend. It is extremely important that you call me as soon as you get this message. I don't care what time it is, day or night, call me immediately."

He ended the message by leaving several numbers. I immediately called his home number. He answered on the second ring.

"Bill, this is Sam. Sorry to be calling so late, but I just got your messages," I said.

"Sam, where have you been? I've been trying to find you since Friday afternoon," he said.

"Out of town. What's the problem?" I said.

"Listen, it's too late to go into it now, meet me at

your office at 8:00 tomorrow morning,'' he said. It was an order, not a request.

''Alright. But what's this about?'' I said.

''Let's just talk about in the morning. I'll have Lieutenant James from the Wasatch PD with me. See you in the morning,'' he said and hung up without giving me a chance to reply.

I went over and over in my mind what could be so important that Bill would try to track me down so hard over Labor Day weekend. And why he would need a Lieutenant from the Wasatch City PD to be in the meeting?

It was after 1:00 when I finally went to bed, but my rest that night was fitful.

I WAS IN my office at 6:45 trying to focus on my work, but my mind was continually pulled back to the previous night's conversation with Bill Nelson. Finally, just before 8:00 there came a polite knock at my open office door and Bill Nelson walked in with a man in an ill-fitted navy blue suit.

''How are you, Sam?'' Bill said.

''I'm good, have a seat,'' I said, indicating the chairs in front of my desk.

''Sam McKall, this is Lieutenant Fred James of the Wasatch City police,'' Bill said before taking his seat.

''Nice to meet you, Lieutenant,'' I said as we shook hands. Lt. James was a short man, a full head shorter than me, with closely cropped blond hair and a handlebar mustache.

"Likewise," James said, taking the seat nearest the window.

"Last Thursday, you had lunch with Valerie Turpin, did you not, Sam?" Bill said.

"I did." I gave a nod with my answer. "Has something happened to her?" I added after a second's thought. The panic in my voice was more than evident.

"No, she's fine," Bill said.

"Thank goodness, she told me about what's been going on. I've been worried," I said.

"That's frankly why we are here," he said.

"Well, if I can—"

"At lunch you asked her about some information Ralf Voss had sent her," Bill said, cutting me off mid-sentence.

"That's right," I said, perplexed by tone of his voice.

"Why?" he asked.

"Why what?" I said.

"What is your interest in that information?" the Lieutenant spoke for the first time.

"Well as far as I understand, it had to do with a plan he had to stop the nuclear waste dump on the Pishute Reservation. Knowing Senator Voss, it must have been a good plan and I wanted to see if there was something there we could use," I said.

"Ms. Turpin explained to you that her office had been vandalized by a stalker?" the Lieutenant said.

"She did."

"Until your conversation with her, she had thought

that the only thing stolen from her office was a gym bag with dirty workout clothes."

"That is what she told me."

"Yes, but now we have discovered one other thing," the Lieutenant was in full control now. Bill sat quietly looking at his hands.

"And that is?" I said.

"The file you requested from her," he said.

"The information Voss sent her?" I said.

"That's right. Can you tell me what was in that file?" the Lieutenant said.

"I don't know what was in it. That's why I asked to see it."

"How did you even learn the file existed?"

I thought about not answering that question but realized that I had already told Valerie and that she had likely relayed the information to them.

"Wayne Smith of the *Capitol Times* told me about it," I said.

"And your contention is that you had no knowledge what was contained in that file, Mr. McKall?" he said, leaning forward in his chair with one hand on my desk, the other on his knee.

"I'm not contending anything, Lieutenant James. I am telling you a fact," I said, leaning forward in my chair.

"Where do you most often shop for groceries?" he asked with a silly grin on his face.

"What?"

The question seemed so totally irrelevant that I couldn't process it.

"Where do you shop for groceries? It's a simple question," he said mockingly slowly.

"The Albertson's on 8th South and 8th East," I said.

"Would it surprise you to learn that several of the threatening phone calls Ms. Turpin has received came from the pay phone right outside that store?" he said.

"Yes. Yes it—"

"And your car Mister McKall. What kind of car do you drive?" he said.

"A 1998 Jeep Cherokee," I said. I could feel my face turning red as the anger began to build up inside me. I kept telling myself this was no time to lose control. Obviously there had been some mistake.

"Color?"

"Burgundy."

"I suppose you would be equally unsurprised to learn that we have had reports that a vehicle matching that exact description was seen hanging around Ms. Turpin's neighborhood."

"Bill, what is he talking about?" I turned my attention to Bill, trying to get a grip on what was happening.

"Sam, I think you should just answer the Lieutenant's questions," he said, looking up from his hands for the first time since the Lieutenant had taken over.

"This is ridiculous," I said.

The Lieutenant shrugged his shoulders as if to say, "How do you know that?"

"I'm sure you know by now that my fingerprints are not on the pay phone at Albertson's," I said.

"We checked as a matter of formality, but I knew we would not find anything. Whoever is making these calls is smart enough not to leave fingerprints on a pay phone used to commit a crime."

"Yet I am, in your opinion, dumb enough to drive to Valerie's neighborhood in my own vehicle for the purpose of stalking her?"

Again the shrug.

I felt sick, physically sick. So many thoughts were swirling through my head I could not make sense of any of them. I felt as though any second I was going to throw up all over my desk. I fought hard to gather my thoughts.

"Why, if I stole the Voss file, would I raise suspicions by asking Valerie to give it to me?" I said, attacking what occurred to me as the weakest link.

"I don't know. Maybe you thought it would deflect suspicion. Maybe you thought there was more, that you didn't get it all. Maybe you wanted to make sure you got it all. Could be a million reasons," he said, making a point of showing that while I was on the verge of full-scale panic he was coolly under control.

I decided to just shut up and answer only the questions I was asked. I wanted—no, needed—this to end.

The room was silent. Bill had gone back to looking at his hands.

"Is there anything else, Lieutenant?" I asked.

"Yes, Mr. McKall, don't leave town without checking with us," he said as he stood to leave.

"Lieutenant James, you have my full and complete cooperation, but I will go and come as I please. Thank you for coming by, gentlemen,'' I said. Bill and the Lieutenant exchanged glances.

''Listen Sam, just do everyone a favor and let the Lieutenant know your whereabouts,'' Bill said.

''Bill, get out of my office. I've got work to do if you don't mind,'' I said.

''Alright Sam, I'm just trying to help. I'm your friend,'' Bill said.

I simply ignored him. A second later they were gone.

I waited until I was sure they were completely out of our offices and I started dialing Smitty.

''News Room, Smitty,'' he said.

''Smitty, Sam.'' I said.

''Sammy, where have—''

''We need to meet right now. Alone.''

''What's going on?'' he could tell I was concerned about something.

''Now, Smitty!''

''Okay I'm leaving right now. Where?''

''Meet me right at the entrance to Memory Grove,'' I said.

''I'll be there in 10 minutes,'' he said and hung up the phone.

MEMORY GROVE IS a set of walking and jogging trails just east of the Capitol. I left my desk the second I hung up the phone and walked over to meet Smitty. He joined me in five minutes.

''What's going on, Sam?'' he said as he walked into earshot.

"Do you know what's been happening to Valerie Turpin, in Legislative Research?"

"The stalker, you mean?"

"Yes. The police think I'm the stalker."

"What?" Smitty said, stopping dead in his tracks.

"That's right. And it looks like a...what do you call it...a set-up," I said.

"What?" Smitty was truly bewildered.

"Remember, you told me about Voss opening that bill file?"

"Right."

"Well last Thursday, I had lunch with her and asked her to get a look at it, thinking there may be something useful in it. Turns out it was the only thing stolen when the stalker broke into her office. That and a gym bag."

"Say that again," Smitty said.

"The stalker stole Voss's nuke file." I reduced it to the simplest form.

"I got that, but why do they think it was you?"

"Well, apparently Valerie never realized it was gone until I asked to see it," I said.

"That hardly makes you the stalker."

"Yes, but several of the threatening calls Valerie got were made from the grocery store where I shop. And they've had calls from people who have seen a vehicle matching the description of my Cherokee in Valerie's neighborhood."

"You've got to be kidding me," Smitty said.

"Believe me, I wish I were. But I'm telling you

the truth. Bill Nelson and a Lieutenant Fred James were in my office not ten minutes ago,'' I said, pointing in the direction of my office.

''Fred James?'' he said with raised eyebrows.

''That's the one. Why?'' I said.

''That guy's a jerk. Doesn't have many friends on the force,'' he said.

''How do you know that?'' I said without thinking.

Smitty just looked at me and shrugged his shoulders.

''Maybe now you'll believe me when I tell you there is something more to this than coincidence,'' Smitty said. I had not considered it yet, but yes, his conspiracy theory was looking much more credible to me than it had an hour ago.

''Tell me what happened, word for word,'' Smitty said.

As nearly as I could I told him everything that had happened since the phone call from Bill Nelson the night before.

''You talked to Beckstead about this yet?'' he said after I had finished.

''Not yet, I'm sure Bill's in his office right now,'' I said.

''You better be the next one in there. I'll sit on it of course, but I can't stop anybody else,'' he said, referring to another problem I had not even thought of yet. One hint of this in the press and I was done for. Again my stomach seized as I fought back the urge to vomit. Everything I had ever worked for was hanging by a thread it seemed. If the media got one whiff of this I would be through. Even if I was completely exonerated, the damage done by the suspicion alone would be real and lasting. I had seen it happen too many times to believe it wasn't true.

Beckstead, I knew, would stand by me only as long as it was in his best interest. And the minute it was in the media, it would no longer be in his best interest. My stomach was wrenching in earnest.

I felt trapped.

There was no way out that I could see. Suddenly, I felt lightheaded.

"You alright, Sam? Here, let's sit down," Smitty said, taking my arm and directing me to a nearby bench. From his coat pocket he produced a flask and removed the cap.

"Here, take a swallow of this," he said, putting it in my mouth. Dazed, I took a swallow. Not being much of a drinker, that was all it took. Knocking the flask out of my mouth, I leaned over behind the bench and threw up.

"Sorry, Sam. You alright?" Smitty said, picking up the flask while patting me on the back.

"Yeah, I'm fine," I lied. "What do we do now?"

"You get yourself together and go talk to Beckstead. I'll start discreetly nosing around the police department to see what I can learn," he said.

"Okay," I said.

"There's one other thing, Sam. They probably got enough for a search warrant. You should hire a lawyer just in case they do."

That sent me for another trip behind the bench.

I GATHERED MYSELF as best I could, said good-bye to Smitty, and found my way to a bathroom in the basement of the capitol. I rinsed my mouth out several times with water and washed my face over and over again with cold water. Gradually the dizziness I had been feeling subsided and I could walk without feeling as though I was going to fall over at any moment. I took a seat in one of the stalls and took several deep breaths. Finally when I convinced myself that I was feeling as good as I was likely to feel for a while, I made my way back up to the Governor's office.

"Sam, the Governor is looking for you," the receptionist at the front desk said as I walked in.

"Thank you," I replied.

I walked into his office where his secretary said the same thing to me. I walked into his back office unannounced. He was standing behind his desk looking out a west-facing window.

"Just had a very interesting visit from Bill Nelson," he said without turning around.

"I know," I said, wanting to sit down but opting to stand as long as he was.

"What the hell's going on?" he said turning from the window and focusing on me.

"That is what I'd like to know, Governor—"

"Are you stalking this Turpin woman or not?" he said, the anger rising in his voice.

"Of course not. No. Thank you for your confidence," I said, feeling my own anger begin to surge.

"I'm just looking out for this administration, something you apparently haven't been doing," he said.

"Listen, just calm down for a minute and let me explain what happened," I said.

"Calm down? *Calm down?* I've worked too hard to get here, spent too much of my own money getting elected to this office to watch you destroy it out from under me."

"Just sit down and let me explain," I said.

Jerking his chair from under his desk, he sat down and stared at me, daring me to explain. I sat on a sofa next to his desk and started from the very beginning, laying the whole thing out for him, from the time Smitty called for my help until Bill and Lieutenant left my office.

"So you're being set up. That's your story?" he said.

"That's not my 'story.' That's what's happening," I said.

"I can't help but notice that if you had been tending to business here instead of playing reporter in San Francisco, none of this would have ever happened. Would it?"

"No, Governor, that's not actually true either. What really raised suspicion is when I asked for Senator Voss's file. And the one and only reason I did that was the thought that he might help us come up with an idea on how to stop this nuke dump," I said, just at the edge of raising my voice.

"Let me explain something to you. You're gone from this office the minute, no the second this hits the press. Period. End of story. But if by some miracle you manage to keep this thing out of the media and it blows over somehow...well we'll talk about that then. Is that clear?'' he said, standing from his chair to let me know that he was through discussing the matter.

''Very,'' I said as I stood.

''And let me say one other thing. Just so we are both clear. The only reason I am not showing you the door this second is the very slight chance that this won't make the papers and I won't have to clean up your mess up. That is the only reason. Understood?''

''Crystal clear.'' And frankly it could not have been more so.

TWELVE

IT WAS JUST AFTER 1:00 in the afternoon. Despite having thrown up what little breakfast I had eaten, I was not at all hungry. The thought of eating anything made me nauseous.

I began weighing in my mind whether or not I should take Smitty's advice and hire a criminal defense lawyer. On one hand, I was the target of a criminal investigation. On the other hand, I had nothing to hide. I may have been the target of a set-up, but there was nothing either at my house or in my office that would corroborate that. Hiring an attorney, no matter what anybody says, makes you look guilty. So after careful consideration I decided against it.

The worst thing about my situation was the helplessness of it. I could not think of one thing I could do to help myself. I thought about calling Valerie, but decided that that could only make things worse. It made me ill every time I considered the fact that she probably now thought of me as her stalker. In the four hours since Bill Nelson and Lt. James had walked through my office door, my life had been turned completely upside-down and continued to shake and quiver as though it were preparing for another tumble.

Then it dawned on me that what was likely to be the most unpleasant part of what was easily the worst day of my life lay ahead—I had to call Tracey. On the unlikely chance that this would make the papers, I had to make sure that she heard it from me first. I knew her reaction would be 180 degrees from the Governor's, but still it was not going to be any fun to tell her that her new boyfriend was thought by the police to be a dangerous and deranged stalker.

"OH HI, SAM. I have been thinking about you all day." I found Tracey at her apartment in D.C. And even though I had been dreading the call, just hearing her voice made me feel better.

"I can't tell you how much I miss you," I said.

"Is there something wrong?" she asked and I could hear the concern in her voice.

"Yes, and you're not going to believe it either. I can't believe it and I am living through it."

"What? What is it?"

I had not even mentioned to Tracey what Smitty and I had done while we were in Maine. Work never came up. Until this morning I had believed that Smitty was off on some wild goose chase. Even if we had talked about work, I was not sure it would have occurred to me to tell her what was going on with the Leapingdeer story.

So, for the second time that day, I related the whole story from start to finish.

"This is a joke, right?" She said even though she could tell by the tone of my voice that it wasn't.

"It's a nightmare," I said. "My stomach has been in a dime-sized knot all day. I don't know what to do."

"There must be something you can do," she said, beginning to feel some of the frustration I had been feeling all day.

"Smitty thinks it's connected to the nuclear story he's working on," I said.

"Has to be, that's the only common thread. Isn't it?"

"I'm not thinking that clearly, but it is the only one I can see. Smitty is convinced it is. Course, he was absolutely convinced the whole thing was some kind of conspiracy before all this happened."

"But he didn't see anything like this coming. Did he?" she asked.

"Well if he's right, we're dealing with someone who would kill an 80-year-old woman in her shower. Setting me up as a stalker shouldn't be too much of a stretch for him. Her. Whoever it is," I said.

"Yeah, I guess you're right. But it's one thing to sneak into someone's house and kill them in the shower and tamper with someone's brakes. And it is another thing to set up this elaborate stalker scheme. That takes quite a bit more sophistication. Don't you think?"

"Question is, what do you do about it?" I said.

"You should help Smitty get to the bottom of it all. What else can you do?"

"That's about it," I said and exhaled long and deep.

"How are you holding up?" she asked after I had finished.

"Not very well, I'm afraid," I said.

"It's nice of Beckstead to stand by you like that," she said, her voice dripping with sarcasm. "I never have liked that guy. I don't think Senator Hansen does either."

"I don't think he's on anybody's man-of-the-year list. But, if you really think about it you can't blame him. If this thing goes public, the person most affected by it, after me, will be him. He's smart enough to know that his numbers are so tenuous now that harboring a known stalker will probably be enough to finish him off. Regardless of what happens to this nuke dump," I said.

"That's right, and if he were anything but a blowhard with a neck-sized I.Q. he'd realize that his best chance of avoiding the fall-out, pun intended, is to help you resolve this situation as quickly as possible," she said.

"That's right, and there's only one reason why he wouldn't do that," I said.

"He's an idiot."

"No, there's another reason," I said, not wanting to say it out loud.

"He thinks you may have done it." It sounded worse than I imagined.

"That's right. And if he helps me, it looks like he was trying to cover it up."

"That is the dumbest thing I've ever heard," she said. Her faith in me was reassuring.

"Look, Beckstead is no Rhodes Scholar. I'll give you that. But he is a savvy politician in his own way and he's smart enough to do the math on this and like it or not, that is one of the variables he has factored in."

"His loyalty is inspiring," she said almost to herself.

"Politics is a business of shifting alliances. And at times like this you learn what a cold hard fact that is," I said.

"I can't believe you're defending him," she said.

"I'm not defending him," I said. "Just trying to figure out what I'm up against."

ALTHOUGH I HAD DREADED calling Tracey, I felt much better after having talked to her. It had provided the first indication all day that all might not be lost.

I decided the first thing I should do is make a copy of everything I had in my office related to this Nuke Dump. That way, if I was arrested, at least I would still have copies to work from.

I WAS BACK in my office having made the last of the copies when Smitty called and asked me to meet him at Lucky's. It was after 7:00 when we met.

Smitty was working on a scotch and soda.

"How are you?" he asked as I sat down.

"Been better. What do you got?"

"Not a lot but I do have the dates and times these calls were made from Albertson's. Let's go over them and see if you have an alibi,'' he said, removing a notebook from his coat pocket.

''Where do you get information like that?'' I asked.

After hearing my question, he gave me the you-know-better-than-to-ask-me-that look. And he was right, I did.

''They don't have everything yet. Apparently there was another call made this weekend but they don't have the information on that one yet. Okay,'' he said, looking at his notes, ''First call from Albertson's was...''

ONE BY ONE he went over the dates. My heart was racing and my throat tightening when he read the last date and I realized that all three of these calls were made at about the time I was actually shopping in the store. I was inside shopping while someone was outside at the pay phone making the calls. I was really scared when I realized how easy it was going to be for them to prove it. I do almost all my shopping with a credit card that deducts the money I spend directly from my checking account. A date and time of each purchase is safely stored in my bank's computer just waiting to be discovered.

It would only be a matter of time before it was.

''You have got to be kidding me, Sam,'' Smitty said after I had explained my shopping habits to him.

''I wish I were,'' I said.

''You mean somebody followed you to the store, waited on you to go in, and made the calls,'' he said.

"That's what it looks like to me," I said, trying to catch my breath.

"Did you hire a lawyer like I said?"

"Not yet."

"You better get on it. Last thing you want to happen is for them to see those bank records," he said.

"This is unbelievable. I am innocent and you are telling me I should withhold evidence from the police?" I said.

"You tell me, Sammy. What's our friend Lieutenant James going to think, when he gets a look at them? This guy's got it in for you Sam, that's what I'm told anyway."

"That was pretty obvious when he was in my office," I said.

"I'll tell you this, I've seen arrest warrants issued on a lot less than what those bank records will provide them. But you do have one thing going for you. The order has come down from the top to be very careful in the way they handle you. They don't want any mistakes."

"How is that going to help me?" I said.

"Probably means that they're going to wait until they have more evidence than they normally would before they issue an arrest warrant," he said. "Buys us a little time."

"That's something, I guess."

"It's the best we are going to get for right now, I'm afraid. Let me show you something." He reached into his suit coat pocket and pulled a small rubber hose and handed it to me.

It was dry and cracked with small pieces of rubber flaking off in my hands.

"That's a brake line," he said. "Bought it this morning."

"At a junk yard?" I said.

"No, this is brand new."

"It doesn't look it," I said as I handed it back to him and dusted off my hands.

"That's because I sprayed it with some stuff called 'Gum-go.' They use it in schools to remove gum from the carpet. Freezes the gum rock hard, so they can just chip it away."

"That was brand-new this morning?"

"Brand spanking," he said.

"Amazing."

"Extreme cold. That's what my mechanic said this morning and he was right," Smitty said, obviously proud of himself.

"That could explain Jeff's first accident. But the brakes were working fine for the second one," I said.

"Maybe not," he said with a sly smile.

"I hate to break it to you Smitty, but they were. The police showed me pictures of the skid marks Jeff left on the road."

"I asked my mechanic about that as well, and he told me that if you put a little oil in the brake's master cylinder that it would cause the brakes to completely lock up. So Jeff is driving down a mountain road. Maybe going a little fast as he starts taking a sharp corner. Touches his brake to slow down just a little bit and WHAM. The brakes lock up. He loses control of the car. It rolls off the road and down the hillside,'' he said, using his hands to demonstrate the action of the car as it rolled.

''Oil in the master cylinder?'' I said.

''That's what my mechanic says. Takes less than a minute once you get the hood up.''

''Could be on to something.''

THIRTEEN

IT WAS ABOUT 10:00 p.m. when I lugged a box full of nuke dump documents into my apartment. The maid service had been by and the place was spotlessly clean. I carried the documents into the bedroom in order to begin the tedious process of reading through them. I sat them down beside my nightstand and noticed something out of the corner of my eye on my bed. It was a black canvas bag. My first thought was that it was something the cleaning service must have found under my bed and did not know what to do with.

Pulling to the edge of the bed, I unzipped it and was greeted by a damp musty smell. Inside was a set of women's workout clothes and shoes. When I realized what it was, I actually jumped away from it as though it was a deadly snake.

This was Valerie Turpin's gym bag, stolen from her office. Someone had broken into my apartment and left it on my bed. My chest was tight, my heart was racing, I was finding it hard to breathe. I was as close to a full-scale panic as I had been all day. I left the room and shut the door. Walking into the bathroom, I splashed some water on my face and forced myself to breathe slowly and deeply. Gradually my heart rate slowed to something more human.

My first rational thought was to call the police. I walked over and started dialing the number before hanging up. Lt. James had said that one of the reasons I might have asked for the Voss file was to deflect suspicion that I had stolen it. This would only raise their suspicions that much more. But on the other hand, I thought, suppose they kick down my door in the morning with a search warrant, the gym bag would be the icing on the cake. Then my only defense would be, "I was going to call, honest I was."

I decided to err on the side of what was going to keep this thing out of the newspapers the longest and that was clearly not calling the police, at least not yet.

But just in case the police did show up with a search warrant, I needed to get the bag out of my house. But where and how? I was pretty sure that whoever was doing this to me was aware of all my moves. They knew when I went shopping. They knew when I was and wasn't at home. For all I knew I was being watched twenty-four hours a day. I felt like I had to get it out of my house immediately, but where could I go this time of night?

AFTER CHANGING INTO a pair of jeans, a t-shirt and a baseball cap, I unpacked the box I had carried the documents in with and stuffed the gym bag in. Then placed enough of the documents on top to obscure the box's true cargo. Then I carried it back out to my car and up to the Capitol. As casually as possible I tried to survey the street to determine if I was being followed, but even in my paranoid state I couldn't see anything I thought was out of the ordinary. Even so, I decided not to take any chances. It was best to assume that I was being followed and make the decisions based on that probability.

As nonchalantly as I could, I drove toward the Capitol, parked in my assigned spot and walked into the building the way I normally do. Still no sign of a tail. All the doors were locked as they always are this time of night. I used a combination of traditional and electronic keys to get into the Capitol, each door locking automatically behind me, and worked my way over to the Governor's office. Once in the office, I called a cab to meet me at the corner of Main Street and North Temple. Then using a back entrance rarely used by anyone other than the Governor's security, I exited the Capitol on the west side, hoping that whoever was following me would simply wait for me to come out the same way I came in.

Cautiously, I walked across the Capitol lawn, staying in the shadows as much as possible until I reached Main Street. Once on Main, I walked as casually as I could toward North Temple where a cab was waiting.

"You call a cab?" said the white-haired driver as I opened his back door and slid in.

"I did. Bus station please," I said and without another word he dropped the meter and drove off.

A few minutes later he delivered me to the front

of the bus station. I paid him his fare and a forgettable tip and sent him on his way.

I walked into the bus station and directly over to the pay-per-use lockers. Paying enough for a month, I removed the bag from the box and shoved it into the locker and locked it away. Slipping the key into my pocket and walking out the front door, I then caught another cab to the corner of Main and North Temple. I paid the driver, tipped appropriately and walked back to the Capitol. In through the back way and up to the office, I filled the box again with miscellaneous documents and headed for my car. I checked my watch before walking out of the building and into the parking lot. Thirty-five minutes. The whole thing had taken thirty-five minutes, not enough time, I hoped, to raise the curiosity of whoever might be following me.

Ten minutes later I walked into my apartment. I walked into my laundry room and buried the key in a box of laundry soap. As I was wiping the soap particles from my hands the phone rang. I looked at my watch, 1:15 a.m. Too late for Tracey. I picked it up on the second ring.

"Hello," I said.

"Sam, this is Smitty."

"Smitty? You all right?"

"I need you to come bail me out of jail."

"What?" I said.

"I'm at the Wasatch County jail. You're not going to believe this. I—"

"Don't tell me over the phone. Let's talk when I

pick you up.'' I was wondering if my phone was now bugged. ''How much money do I need to bail you out?'

''Six hundred cash,'' he said.

''See you in thirty minutes,'' I said and hung up the phone.

THIRTY MINUTES LATER I had stopped by my cash machine and arrived at the jail. I posted the bail and waited in a small waiting room in the lower level of the jail.

''Wasn't that bad,'' a youngish sheriff's deputy said to another. Both were stationed behind a small counter. ''Yeah, car flipped four times, but all three passengers lived, their stuff was spread for at least 300 yards up and down the interstate.''

Gradually, I blocked out the two officers and focused again on my problems. The kiss I had shared with Tracey at the Portland airport less than thirty-six hours ago seemed to be something that had happened to another person. I was beginning to feel lightheaded and dizzy again. I closed my eyes and leaned my head against the filthy wall behind my chair.

''HEY BUDDY, you alright?'' I heard a voice saying.

''Hey buddy,'' he said again before I realized he was talking to me. I snapped back to reality and realized I was shaking all over. The two officers behind the counter were looking at me as though I were some strung-out junkie.

''Yeah I'm fine, I just have a fever,'' I lied.

"Right," one said and they both laughed.

Just as I was about to slip back into my own little world, I heard a loud buzz, a door to the side of the counter opened and out walked Smitty. He looked as bad as I felt.

"What happened, Smitty?" I said.

He pointed to the door, indicating he wanted to wait until we were outside to talk.

Once outside the jail, Smitty exhaled in one long breath.

"DUI. They picked me up for a DUI," he said.

"DUI. I was afraid it might be something else," I said.

"I think it was," he said.

"What do you mean?"

"I'd been drinking. I'd been drinking too much I admit that. But these guys didn't pull me over for speeding or reckless driving. They were waiting on me. The second I turned onto my street, their lights came on and they pulled me over. I mean they were there waiting on me. Just waiting," I said.

I don't know how drunk he had been, but he was sober now.

"They do a breathalyzer on you?" I asked.

"Point oh nine," he said.

"What's the legal limit?"

"Point oh eight. They got me dead to rights," he said.

"And they were there waiting on you?" I said. Less than 18 hours ago I would have laughed him out of my Jeep with a story like that, but not anymore. I believed every word.

"Tell me how to get to your house," I said and he did.

"Course this will be all over the news tomorrow," he said as soon as we were out of the car. "*Times* won't cover it but everyone else will."

I have always suspected that there was a lot of professional jealousy among Smitty's peers over his success and I imagined that they would not let this chance to undermine his credibility pass without strong comment and a full measure of righteous indignation.

"While you were being booked into the county jail, guess what I found waiting for me at the apartment?"

"What?"

"The gym bag stolen from Valerie Turpin's office," I said under my breath as though there might be someone hiding behind the trees in Smitty's yard.

"Unbelievable," he said, the disbelief written all over his face.

"Believe it. Somebody broke into my apartment and just left the bag sitting on my bed."

Smitty began shaking his head slowly from side to side as he considered everything.

"I'm sorry I ever doubted your conspiracy theory, but it looks like we are up against something big. Bigger than the two of us anyway," I said.

"Things always look bigger than they really are when they're hanging over you. We got to find a way to get out from under this thing," Smitty said.

"We have no idea who these people are, Smitty. They, on the other hand, know where and when I go shopping and that you had too much to drink tonight. They know everything, we know nothing," I said, feeling the shakes begin to come on again.

"That's not true," Smitty said defiantly. "We know they're out there. I mean they've tipped their hand to us a little bit. Haven't they?" he said.

"Yeah, by showing us they can destroy our lives. That's a pretty strong hand," I said.

"And that is a fundamental strategy in game theory. Sometimes you want your opponent to know your strength, so that they won't do something that is equally damaging to both sides," he said.

"You mean this is all a warning?" I said.

"Could be. I don't know. They know we are on to them and they want to show us what the price is going to be if we expose them," he said.

"Well they have vastly overestimated what we are capable of, because we don't even know who these people are. And we are in absolutely no position to harm them," I said.

"Sam, think about it for a second. It's not going to be very hard to put together a very small list of companies and people who could possibly be behind all this," Smitty said.

I just looked at him with a quizzical look on my face.

"Its simple. Whoever is doing this, is profiting from the deal somehow," he said.

"Wait just one minute, Smitty, you're not about to

tell me that a group of power companies with over a trillion dollars in assets are so desperate for the comparatively little profit they will make on this deal, that they have sanctioned murders to make sure the deal goes through. Are you?'' I said.

''They have to be on the list, but there are others. The tribe is making money on this thing, hundreds of times as much money as they've ever seen out there,'' he said.

''That seems only slightly more plausible and only because they need the money. But I've got to tell you, Beckstead and I met with Jack Longnight and I can tell you that guy is a shrewd politician, but he sure didn't come across as the ringleader of a murder conspiracy,'' I said, remembering how well he had handled the governor. ''Besides, that's too obvious.''

''Don't forget that whoever is doing this has gone to great lengths to make everything that happened look like an accident. They did that because they figured that if anyone became suspicious the trail would lead to them too easily,'' he said.

''We still don't have one single piece of evidence we can point to that would either prove that either of these deaths was a murder,'' I said.

''But we know they were murders and that's what scares them,'' he said.

''And if we ever did come up with any evidence our credibility will be so seriously undermined by them that there is a good chance that no one will believe us,'' I said.

''They can't ignore hard evidence,'' he said.

"Of which we have exactly none," I said, getting a little frustrated.

"Well Sam, what do you want to do? Start typing your confession or help me find some," he said.

I did not want to say anything to him, but the thought of jumping on a plane to some Caribbean island and camping out on a beach until this whole thing blew over had crossed my mind more than once.

"Where do we go from here?" I said as a form of surrender.

"I listened to all of Jeff's tapes today. Finished the last one after you left Lucky's. There was a tape for every day of his last two weeks except for the day he was murdered," he said.

"Anything on them?"

"They are dictations of memos and little jobs he needs his secretary to do. From time to time he'll tell her to mail this or that news story about the project to his mother. Or to pull this or that case that he thinks may be useful in fighting the dump, but never any names or anything like that," he said.

"Did you look at the cases he talks about?"

"I got an intern pulling a copy of all of them and the articles, too. I called Max Reeve and she put me on with his secretary. She said Jeff probably had the tape with him when he crashed. Said Jeff would have the previous day's tape on her desk when she arrived in the morning and she would leave out a replacement tape when she left in the evening," he said.

"So it burned in the crash?" I said.

"Looks that way," he said.

"So what next then?"

"We know the Consortium and Tribe stand to make money on this deal; there are bound to be others. We need to find out who they are and start investigating all of them," he said.

"Alright."

"You've got access to all the public filings the Consortium and the Tribe have made on the dump. You go through those and see what you come up with. Tomorrow morning I start pulling the 10K's and the other SEC filings for the Consortium members and just for kicks I'll see what kind of filings the Tribe has made with the Bureau of Indian Affairs in Washington and start pulling those," he said.

"Sounds good. I have already got all the documents that have been filed to date at my apartment. I copied them before I left the office today. Just in case," I said.

"That's a good boy, Sammy," Smitty said with a smile and a pat to my cheek.

"There is one other thing," I said.

"What's that?"

"You better decide what to say about the DUI thing."

"Not much to say, Sammy. I was out drinking, drank too much and got busted driving home," he said with a shrug.

Life is so easy when you don't have to worry about elections.

It was well after 3:00 a.m. when I arrived back at my apartment. Despite the fact that my life seemed to be on an increasingly slippery slope to ruin, I fell exhausted into bed and was sound asleep in a matter of minutes.

FOURTEEN

I WAS JARRED FROM my sleep at exactly 6:30 the next morning by the grating sound of my alarm clock. I was still desperately tired, I knew I had to get up and get busy, so at 6:45 I dragged myself out of bed and into a hot shower.

Finding I was out of coffee and milk for cold cereal, I decided to have breakfast at Rosie's Bagel & Bean, a small café with patio seating not far from my apartment.

"Let's go, Alice," I said as I put her leash on, "we haven't been to Rosie's in so long, she's going to be mad."

Grabbing a small stack of the nuclear documents I had copied the day before I headed toward the café.

"ALICE. WHERE HAVE you been, my sweetheart?" Rosie said as she saw us approaching. Alice took off in a dead run toward Rosie who was already out from behind the counter and on her knees.

"Hi Rosie. Been out of town," I said after I caught up.

Alice had flopped down on her back so that Rosie would have no trouble scratching her belly.

"I missed my little sweetheart," Rosie said.

"I think she missed you too, Rosie," I said.

"Now, Mr. McKall what can I get for you," she said, grunting as she lifted herself from the floor. Rosie was well into her sixties, maybe fifty pounds overweight and one of the most cheerful people I know.

"I'll have a tall decaf and a poppy seed bagel. And do you still have those doggy bagels?" I asked.

"Of course," said Rosie.

"Two of those and a bowl of water for Alice."

"Coming right up. Have a seat out on the patio and I'll bring it to you," she said.

I paid the well-pierced cashier, picked up a copy of the *Wasatch City Daily Reporter*, the bitter rival of the *Capitol Times*, and found a place in the shade to read their story on Smitty's arrest.

It was particularly brutal and even featured pictures of his mug shots. I was amazed that they were able to get copies before the paper had gone to print. It was clear they enjoyed kicking Smitty when he was down.

And I guess I would be lying if I didn't say that, even after being skewered by Smitty in the pages of the *Capitol Times* on more than one occasion, I did not take the smallest amount of pleasure in the fact the *Daily Reporter* offered him no quarter. One thing was certain: he would have offered them none.

"Here you go Mr. McKall," Rosie said as she served my hot coffee and bagels.

"Thank you."

"Where have you been, why don't you ever come by anymore?" she asked.

"Been out of town on business."

"I see, I see. What do you do with Alice when you're gone?" she asked.

"One of the neighbor boys takes care of her."

"Well, can't he bring Alice by at least?" she asked.

"I guess so. I'll ask him," I said.

"That will be nice," she said and dropped a large chunk of cheddar cheese among the doggie bagels she had just delivered. Alice stopped eating just long enough to roll on her back to get one more belly scratch. Rosie obliged and then made her way back behind the counter.

Setting the newspapers aside, I turned my attention to the documents I had brought from the apartment and started reading. All in all, there were well over a thousand pages that needed to be read.

I stopped only once and that was to call the office to say I would not be in. I lied and said I had a bad case of the stomach flu. By 10:00 a.m. I had finished reading the documents I had brought with me to the café and was feeling considerably better after having eaten a whole bagel with cream cheese and half another. I ordered a coffee for the road and headed back to my apartment.

As I walked, unprompted my thoughts went back to the conversation I had overheard while in the county jail waiting room.

"Yeah, car flipped four times, but all three passen-

gers lived, their stuff was spread for at least three hundred yards up and down the interstate," one of them had said.

It occurred to me how lucky they were and unlucky Jeff Leapingdeer had been. His car flipped four times as well, but he was dead. Not one of the three passengers in that car died. "Worst thing that happened to them is they totaled the car and lost whatever stuff was thrown from the car as it rolled," I thought to myself.

That got me thinking about Jeff's car rolling down the hillside.

"...their stuff was spread for at least three hundred yards up and down the interstate."

"What if the recorder was thrown from the vehicle," I said out loud to myself.

The police had only looked hard enough to find the liquor bottle.

"...three hundred yards up and down the interstate."

What if it had been thrown out on the first roll or flung so far away that an investigator who had already made up his mind about the cause of the accident would have overlooked it.

Without realizing it, I began to walk faster and faster until I was in a dead run to my apartment. Alice was doing her best to keep up. Her little legs were moving faster than they ever had and by the time I reached my apartment building her tongue was practically dragging on the floor. I picked her up and ran up the stairs into my apartment.

"News room, Smitty," he said.

"I enjoyed your story this morning," I said.

"I didn't have a story today."

"I mean the one in the *Daily Reporter*. The picture's very becoming," I said, suddenly feeling better about things.

"Those pricks, they dropped the whole load. I'm just glad my mother's not around to see it," he said.

"Listen we need to talk. Meet me at Lamb's in 15 minutes," I said.

"See you there."

By the time I left, Alice had limped to her bed in the laundry room and was fast asleep.

LAMB'S IS A Wasatch City landmark and a favorite café of the old-time Utah political establishment. Besides good food, it also has the virtue of being only a half a block from Smitty's office.

We arrived at Smitty's almost simultaneously and situated ourselves in one of the corner booths.

We both ordered coffee which the waitress poured immediately. As soon as she left the table Smitty produced the flask from his coat pocket and began removing the cap.

"You're joking, right?" I said, pointing to the flask.

"What?" he said as though I were complaining about his adding cream rather than skim milk.

"Do you really think that's a good idea? Today?" I said.

"Alright, alright," he said, re-tightening the cap and putting it away.

"What do you got?" he said.

"I've read through about a fourth of the documents we have in the Governor's office and there's nothing there so far," I said.

"But..." Smitty said, knowing I wasn't there just to ruin his morning coffee.

"But, I got to thinking about Jeff's tapes. The one for his last day. The secretary said she thought he probably had it with him when he crashed, right?"

"Right."

"What if, but instead of burning up in the flames, it was thrown out of the car before the fire started," I said.

Smitty didn't say anything, but I could see the wheels moving inside his head.

"It might very well still be sitting on that hillside still," I said.

"It might be," he said.

"I'm going to take the rest of the documents I have and jump on a plane to San Francisco. I should be back sometime tomorrow afternoon," I said.

"Good luck," Smitty said as I got up to leave.

I walked out the front door and turned around to come back and leave money for my part of the check. As I did, I saw Smitty pouring a healthy shot of whiskey from his flask into his coffee. Our eyes met. I hesitated for a moment, unsure of what to do, then turned and left.

I MISSED THE 1:00 flight to San Francisco and spent most of the afternoon reading in the airport. The next flight was delayed and by the time I arrived in San Francisco there were only a few minutes of sunlight left. I decided to check myself into a hotel and begin the search of the accident site first thing in the morning.

After checking in, I gave Tracey a call to update her on everything.

"You are going to have to call me more often until this thing blows over," she said after I had updated her.

"I will. But I've been busy and I didn't want to worry you," I said in a half-hearted defense.

"Your first call got me worried. Not hearing from you only makes me more worried," she said and I could see where that would be the case.

"Get this thing worked out," she said, "so we can get together soon." The thought of spending a carefree moment with Tracey seemed like some type of nirvana. Even though it had been less than two days before, that Labor Day in York Beach, it seemed more like an idealized childhood memory than the beginning of a relationship that promised many such moments.

"What I would give to be back on that hammock at your parents' beach house. If I knew then what I know now I would have never left it," I said.

"There'll be plenty of evenings in that hammock, Sam, don't worry," she said.

There was an awkward moment where I felt like telling her I loved her, but the time wasn't right.

"I hope so, Tracey. I hope so. I've got to get on this reading," I said. "I'll call you after I finish looking for that tape."

"I'll be waiting," she said.

FIFTEEN

THE COMBINATION OF being in a hotel room and the target of a criminal investigation did not provide for a good night's sleep. I read until about 2:00 a.m. and nodded off some time after 3:00.

Fortunately, I woke up to a typical San Francisco morning—beautiful on every count. I dragged myself out of bed at about 7:30 and took a long hot shower. After a quick breakfast I read files for another hour before heading out to look for the tape.

Before leaving the hotel I decided to check in with Smitty.

"I'm glad you called. I didn't know where to find you. I got a call from Max Reeve this morning," he said.

"What did she say?"

"She was mugged last night. Not too serious. Stole her purse, gave her a black eye, I think."

"She's alright?" I asked.

"Said she was. Sounded okay to me. But whoever did it used her keys to get into her offices," he said.

"And let me guess. They took something from Jeff's office," I said.

"Well, they didn't steal anything. Security walked

in and scared them off. They can't find anything missing," he said.

"What do you think?" I said.

"I went through that office pretty good. All we found was that folder with the press clippings. Nothing really," he said.

"Why would they risk doing that then?" I said.

"Maybe they just thought he had something."

"Maybe he did have something and we didn't know enough to recognize it," I suggested.

"That's possible, but you know me. I'm suspicious of everything."

"But still."

"Maybe you should go by and see her today," he suggested.

I felt a little awkward about doing it, but under the circumstances I agreed to.

After hanging up with Smitty, I called Max.

"Max, Sam McKall. I heard about the mugging. Are you alright?" I said.

"Yes. I'll be fine. Thank you for asking," she said as though I had asked about a hangnail.

"Have you found anything missing from Jeff's office?" I asked.

"The police have been in there all morning with Jeff's secretary, but no one can say for sure what was in those files. I'll be surprised if they come up with anything definitive," she said.

"Listen, I'm in town. Do you mind if I stop in later this afternoon?"

"Certainly not. I'll look forward to showing off my black eye."

I RENTED A CAR at the hotel and drove out to the crash site. I parked on the shoulder. I could still see the thick black lines left by Jeff's tires. It was very clear to see where his car left the road and where it had finally come to rest; the surrounding earth was scorched and vegetation burned to a black crisp. I started walking in a zigzag pattern parallel to the road, gradually working my way down to the crash. I was in no particular hurry, so I was taking my time, looking carefully in every bush and under each piece of debris and litter. I had been at the site about 30 or 40 minutes when a San Francisco PD car pulled up next to mine and Officer Shultz got out of the passenger's side.

"Mister McKall, I thought I might find you here," he said.

"Good morning, Officer Shultz," I said, more than a little surprised to see him.

"I'm wondering if we might have a word with you," he said.

"Certainly. How can I help you?"

"Why don't we do it downtown?"

"Excuse me?"

"Downtown. We'd like to talk to you downtown."

"About what?" I said, feeling the panic rise.

"It would be better for everybody, I think, if we just waited until we got downtown, Mister McKall."

"Alright," I said, not really feeling as though I had an option.

"Officer Candle here will drive your car down," he said, pointing to his partner, who was still standing by the car.

"Am I under arrest?" I said, actually relieved that I was beginning to feel more angry than panicked.

"No, we just have some questions for you," Shultz said in an unassuming tone. But I wasn't buying it on that particular morning.

"Then I will drive my own car 'downtown'," I said. "Right behind you."

"Make it light on yourself," he said as though he had only been trying to do me a favor.

THIRTY MINUTES LATER I was in an interrogation room that Officer Shultz had escorted me to after we had arrived at the police station.

As I am sure was part of their strategy, they left me there alone with my thoughts for another hour. Watching me, I'm sure, through the two-way mirror which comprised one whole wall.

Finally I got tired of the game. I got up from my chair and without a word or hesitation I walked out of the interrogation room and toward the front door. I was no more than halfway down the hall when I heard footsteps running up behind me.

"Mister McKall, where are you going?" It was the voice of Officer Shultz.

"I came here at your request, because you said you wanted to ask me some questions. But I've been here over an hour now and no one has come in to talk to me. So I'm leaving,'' I said, talking over my shoulder without breaking my stride toward the door.

Officer Shultz, I could tell, was not quite sure how to handle the situation.

''You're just making this more difficult on yourself,'' he said, trying to scare me. It had its desired effect but I didn't let it show.

''You know how to find me,'' I said almost to the door.

''Okay, I think they're ready for you now,'' he said.

''Are you sure?'' I said.

''I am sure,'' he said, then stopped. I turned around and followed him back to the room.

Seconds later I was joined by a man in another bad suit. I wondered if every detective shopped at the same Bad Suit Store.

''Mister McKall, I'm Detective Brown. Sorry to keep you waiting. In a hurry?'' he said. Detective Brown was like his name, average. Average height, average build, average face.

''I am now,'' I said.

''What brings you to San Francisco?'' he said, clearly having decided to first try to be my friend.

''I'm looking into the murder of Jeff Leapingdeer,'' I said.

''Investigating a murder?'' he said.

''That's right,'' he said.

''Officer Shultz tells me Leapingdeer died in a car

accident of his own fault," he said, trying to seem genuinely confused.

"Officer Shultz is either lazy or incompetent."

"Really?" he said as though he might be convinced to see it my way.

"Really. Detective Brown, can we cut to the chase here. It is clear this department does not care about Jeff Leapingdeer or for that matter his murder. So let's just move on."

"On the contrary, we do care about Mr. Leapingdeer. In fact that is why we asked you to come here," he said and stopped as though he was awaiting some response from me.

"And..." I finally said to let him know I had no response.

"What time did you get into San Francisco last night?" he asked, very businesslike all of the sudden.

"About 8:30."

"And where were you at 10:30 last night?"

"In my hotel room."

"Alone?"

"Alone."

"You weren't anywhere near the San Francisco Zoological Gardens then?"

"No I was not. I was in my hotel room."

"And you're just here investigating a murder?" he said, mocking me.

"That's right." I did not rise to the bait.

"Do you know Maxine Reeve?" he asked.

"I do. She was a friend of Jeff's."

"You are aware then that someone mugged her last night," he said.

"Yes I am. I spoke to her this morning," I said.

"Is that your M.O.?" he asked.

"Is what my M.O.?" I asked.

"I had a very interesting conversation with a Lieutenant James this morning, Mister McKall. I believe you have made his acquaintance. He was disappointed you didn't check in with him before you left Wasatch City," he said.

"He should get used to it," I said.

"He told me a sad story about what you have been doing to a Ms...." he referred to his notes, "Yes, Ms. Valerie Turpin. You terrorized her, broke into her office, stole some files. And then politely asked for it a few days later trying to cover yourself. And now you have done the same thing to Maxine Reeve."

"That is ridiculous," I said, out of steam on the stoicism.

"Is it? I don't think so. But this time instead of just breaking into her office, you assaulted her first. Then used her keys to get into the office, thinking you could get in and out without anyone being the wiser. But you got caught. Well, okay, not caught but you had to run. With your plan spoiled you knew obviously we would figure out how you got in and sooner or later we would find out you were back in town. So to cover yourself, you called Ms. Reeve and made plans to pay her a visit."

"I was in Jeff's office, with permission, a week ago. I could have taken anything I wanted to at that time. In fact I could have come back anytime and searched that office with Max's permission,'' I said.

''But not without Max knowing you were in there. You probably spotted something, the first time you were in there and decided that you had to come back and get it, when no one would know you were in there,'' he said, leaning back in his chair and obviously very proud of himself.

''Are you serious?'' I said.

''Very.''

''Let me tell you something, detective. You are way, way off base on this. Not even in the ballpark,'' I said, making a futile attempt to persuade him that he had the wrong guy.

''Let me tell you something, McKall, I don't know what exactly you're into, whether you are some kind of freak or something, or if there's some kind of method to your madness, but if I had on you what they've apparently got on you in Wasatch City, you'd be in one of my cells right now, waiting arraignment.''

SIXTEEN

I COULD NOT GET out of that police station fast enough. I got in my car and drove out of the parking lot as fast as I could. My heart raced; I could feel it pounding against my ribs. The whole thing seemed surreal. Staring across a table from a police detective who is convinced that you are a stalker—there is nothing in life that can prepare you for that. The thought that it would happen to me, not only once but twice in a matter of three days, is one that I had never entertained, not even in my darkest fears.

Gradually, I fought back the panic and used my mobile phone to call Smitty and tell him what had just happened.

"You need to get out of San Francisco ASAP," he said.

"I'm going back to the crash site to finished the search, then I'm on the next flight out of here," I said.

"I've been snooping around the companies in this Consortium. I am not coming up with much. This is a big, big project. We're talking billions, so there's a lot of people and companies which stand to make a lot of money on this deal. The problem is identifying them and it ain't going to be easy,'' he said.

''Or quick,'' I said. It was a hopeless feeling.

''No, but we got to get through it all,'' he said.

''Anything else?''

''Yeah. How would you feel about a trip to Albuquerque?'' he said.

''Albuquerque? Why?''

''Maybe one of us should go talk to Calvin,'' he said, referring to Mary's son who was in prison in New Mexico.

''What good would that do?''

''Probably none, but Mary's friends tell me she stayed in close touch with him. He'd call her several times a week. She wrote letters every day. Said her phone bill was several hundred dollars a month,'' Smitty said.

''If he can talk on the phone, why don't you just call him?'' I said.

''Already tried. Prisoners can call out but you can't call in,'' he said.

''Okay, I'll just change my flight out of here. Instead of coming straight home I'll fly down there tonight and try to see him in the morning,'' I said.

''Sure you don't mind? Probably a waste of time,'' he said, talking me out of the trip he just talked me into.

''It's better than waiting around in Wasatch City for the police to come arrest me,'' I said.

By the time I got back out to the crash site it was after 2:00. I quickly found where I had left off and again began my search. But I kept worrying so much about the evidence that was piling up against me that I found it hard to concentrate. Several times I had to stop and go back over certain areas because I caught myself not paying attention.

I had searched from the road all the way to the crash site with no luck. Below the site the grade got much steeper. I searched as far down as I could and was about to give up when I noticed what looked like a small nylon strap in the top of a small leafy bush of some kind. I carefully made my way down the hillside to the bush, which was close enough to the fire that the leaves were singed, burned and black with ash and smut. There, lodged in its branches was a microtape recorder.

It too, was black and showed signs of being too near the flames. Carefully, I pushed the play button. Nothing. Then I pressed the eject button. But the tape door opened only a fraction of the way. Using my fingernails I opened it the rest of the way.

The tape appeared to be in good condition. I put the tape in my pants pocket and scrambled up the hill to my car.

STOPPING AT the first KMart I could find, I bought a microtape recorder. Back in my car, I ripped open the package like a child on Christmas morning, inserted the batteries and tape and pressed play. First there was an unusually loud hissing sound. Then a person mumbling, almost as if someone had covered the microphone but continued to speak. Anxiously, I listed to every second of the tape waiting for it to clear up, but it never did. To my dismay, in ten minutes of recording there was not even one intelligible word.

My hopes which only moments before had been soaring came crashing down with an emphatic thud.

It was the heat. The heat that rendered the recorder useless must have also damaged the tape. What had only minutes before looked like my first break now appeared to be nothing more than another dead end. It was a devastating blow.

Refusing to concede defeat, I took the tape out of the recorder and shook it, then played it again. I closed my eyes and concentrated on every sound, but still I could not make out anything. I banged the recorder against the dashboard, which did nothing but break the plastic cover off the "stop" button. Then in sheer frustration, I removed the tape from the recorder, got out of my car and threw the recorder across the parking lot. I tried to take some satisfaction in watching it shatter against the black asphalt but there was none.

Then after taking several deep breaths, I got back in the car and headed back to the hotel. At the hotel, I changed my plane reservations to go through Albuquerque and left a message for Smitty, telling him about the tape and that I was sending it to him nonetheless. After getting off the phone I FedExed the tape to Smitty, paid the hotel bill, and caught a cab out to the San Francisco International Airport.

MY FLIGHT ARRIVED at 9:15 in the evening. I found a room at the Wyndham Hotel near the airport and checked in.

I tried calling Smitty at his house and at the paper but got no answer at either place. I had better luck reaching Tracey. I told her about the day's events. It was all so strange I had to convince her that it was true, that these people actually thought I was a stalker. She sensed, I think, that I was tired of worrying about the mess and changed the subject.

"My mother called today to tell me how much she and dad liked you," she said.

"Tell her to stay tuned," I said. "There may be more to come."

"Well, if we handle it the right way," she said in a very serious tone, "she may enjoy having a stalker as a weekend house guest."

"Yes, I'm sure she would enjoy that. She seemed the type."

"Anyway, she is already worried about whether or not you'll be coming for Thanksgiving."

"I think my parents are expecting me to join them at their place in Palm Springs. Since my brother died, I'm the only child," I said.

"Absolutely, that's fine, we can get together afterward," she said.

"No, that's not what I meant. I think we should spend Thanksgiving with my parents."

"Are you sure?"

"I'm sure I don't want you in Maine while I'm in Palm Springs."

"It's a date then."

BY THE TIME I had finished with Tracey and taken a bath I found Smitty at home.

"I found the tape," I said.

"Yeah, I got your message. Did you FedEx it?" he said.

"Yeah, sent it before I left for Albuquerque," I said.

"I got a place down in L.A. I've sent stuff like this to before. I'll send it to them and see what they can do with it," he said.

"You think they can fix it?" I asked, my hopes rising again.

"Had pretty good luck with them before, we'll just have to see what they can do this time," he said. "I guess we better hope they do, 'cause I'm not coming up with anything here."

"Nothing?" I said.

"Nada."

The next morning I got a crash course on prison rules pertaining to inmate visitation. After thinking about it, I felt pretty dumb just walking in and asking to see a prisoner. Turns out, there is a clearance process that can take months to complete.

Considering what I had hoped to get out of talking to Calvin Leapingdeer, it hardly seemed worth the effort, but I called my colleague in the New Mexico Governor's office and asked for his help. We had only a passing acquaintance and he was more than a little interested in what I would need from a prisoner in a New Mexico jail, but in the end he did what I would have done in the same situation. He made the calls, got me in, and politely let me know that I owed him a favor. I did not bother telling him that I might not long be in a position to do him any favors. I simply thanked him and headed back out to Los Lunas, New Mexico, the home of the Central New Mexico Correctional Facility.

This time I was treated with every courtesy that could be afforded a smug little political hack that had gone over their heads to circumvent the process. After producing a picture ID and signing this and that, I was escorted into a room with a long conference table dividing the room into two equal parts.

"Have a seat here. Leapingdeer will be here in a minute. Nothing goes over the partition," he said, pointing to an eighteen-inch wooden partition that divided the visitor half of the table from the prisoner half.

"Got it. Thank you," I said but he had already turned his back and headed for his post.

I waited for fifteen minutes before a guard brought in a man about my age wearing an orange jumpsuit pulled only to his waist and a dingy white T-shirt that was at least three sizes too small.

Calvin was not tall, only about 5'7", but he was lean and sinewy. Muscles rippled up his forearm with the slightest move of his fingers. Every visible part of his body, except his face, was tattooed. His hair was long and combed straight back.

The guard brought him to the chair across from mine.

"Thank you for seeing me, Mr. Leapingdeer," I said, not sure whether or not he had a choice.

"Supposed to be my yard time," he said.

"I'm sorry to keep you from it, I just have a few questions—"

"Look man, I already told you people I don't know where any bodies are buried. I don't want any deals. Just leave me alone. Every time one of you people shows up it causes me trouble. Today ain't going to be no different," he said.

"Mr. Leapingdeer, I am not here about you. I'm here about your mother," I said.

"Well, I know about the will already. So I'm up outta here," he said and got up to leave.

"I'm not here about the will either. I think she and Jeff may have been murdered," I said.

He stopped, gave me a puzzled look and sat back down.

"Say again?" he said.

"I'm looking into it," I said.

"Who?" he said.

"I'm with the Governor's off—"

"Who did it?" he said over my sentence.

"I don't know. I think it my have been connected somehow to a nuclear waste dump that is being proposed out on the reservation. Have you heard about it?" I said.

"Yeah, she used to talk about it in her letters and when she'd call and stuff," he said.

"What'd she say?"

"She was torn over it. She was getting a lot of

pressure from Longnight and his kind to support it. But Jeff, he was pushing just as hard the other way."

"Anybody ever threaten her?" I said.

"Not that I know about. She would have never told me if there was. Afraid of what I might do." I could understand her concern.

"I got a letter from her after she had died, said she had decided to change her vote," he said.

"Change her vote?"

"Yeah, I guess Jeff had won out. Said the Tribe really needed the money and jobs, but this wasn't the right way. I called her right after I got the letter, but there was no answer. When I heard the next day I figured..." he let his sentence trail off.

"Anything else in the letter?"

"Not really, she wasn't looking forward to telling Jack Longnight, that's all," he said.

"Do you still have this letter?"

"Yeah."

I thought about asking the guard to take him back to his cell to get it, but decided that was not going to happen.

"Could I get you to mail me a copy of it?" I asked instead.

"You think somebody murdered her over this," he said.

"It is beginning to look more and more like it," I said.

"Sure, I'll mail it to you."

I got up and walked over to the guard sitting on a

stool at the end of the table. I showed him a business card with my home address written on it.

"Can I give this to him?" I asked.

He shrugged his shoulders by way of giving permission.

I walked back and handed Calvin the card.

"Send it to my home address," I said as I extended the card across the partition.

"Carton of cigarettes ought to cover my out of pockets," he said as he slid the card into his pocket.

Took me a second to realize what he was talking about.

"What's your brand," I said.

"Camels without."

"Without?"

"Filters."

"I'll mail 'em to you as soon as I leave here," I said.

"I'll send the letter when I get 'em."

TWO HOURS LATER the carton of Camels was on its way to Calvin and I was on my way back to Wasatch City. I had finished reading all of the documents submitted by the Tribe and the Consortium to the Nuclear Regulatory Commission and the Bureau of Indian Affairs. Nothing had raised any suspicions. All of the filings were filled out very precisely and completely and signed by both Jack Longnight for the Tribe and Tom Griggs of the Consortium. I am sure our lawyers would find plenty of things to argue over, but I could find nothing.

The last thing I had to read was the long-term lease between the Tribe and the Consortium. On the surface everything about the lease seemed to be in order. I had not seen a lot of leases in my life, but this one appeared to be nothing out of the ordinary. But still there was something that did not seem to add up. Literally.

The project that was talked about in the Nuclear Regulatory Commission documents, was 844 acres larger than the amount of land being leased by the Consortium from the Tribe.

Eight hundred and forty-four acres. I searched, but could not find any reason for the discrepancy. I considered whether or not it was a mistake and I could not rule it out, although it did seem unlikely. I mean, if an uninitiated layman like myself could spot it, certainly, if it were a mistake, it would have been caught by someone else.

"It's probably nothing," I said to myself.

But I hoped it was something.

SEVENTEEN

AS I WAS DRIVING in from the airport, I was beginning to see, ever so faintly, what might be a light at the end of the tunnel. We finally had a few things to work on now.

The first thing, and perhaps the most promising, was the tape. Hopefully, Jeff would have left a record of whatever he learned on that tape. Smitty had had the tape all day and with any luck was reclaiming what Jeff had recorded on it.

Next, I had the letter from Mary to Calvin confirming that she had changed her mind about supporting the dump and that she was nervous about telling Jack Longnight. At a minimum this provided a motive for why someone supporting the project would have wanted to see her dead.

Then there was the discrepancy in the acreage leased and the amount of acreage needed for the project.

I had tried to get in touch with Smitty, but he was not at his desk, at home or at Lucky's. Hopeful, he had learned something from Jeff's tape and was off chasing it down. I decided to call Tom Griggs about the acreage problem and save my visit to Jack Longnight until after I had spoken to Smitty.

I drove as fast as I could to my office where I had Griggs' business card. The Consortium had opened an office in Wasatch City and hopefully I could catch him there before he left for the day.

It was an awkward moment walking in the front door and to my office. Clearly rumors were swirling around the office about me and people were surprised to see me, embarrassed to be caught staring at me and questioning whether their boss lived a perverted double life. I tried to act as natural as I could as I made my way back to my office and shut the door behind me. It was a sick feeling.

I had hired most of the people in that office and known most of them well before that. Counted them as friends. It was evident in their eyes and in their body language that they were ready to assume the worst. In the two days since the accusations were made, I had not received one inter-office e-mail, no one from the staff had left me a voice mail, no memos were left on my desk requiring my action. Nothing. Nobody. It made me wonder that even if by some miracle I was able to keep it out of the paper, if I would ever be free from the taint of these suspicions. A very depressing thought.

I shook my head as if to dislodge the thought, found Tom Griggs' business card and dialed his office number.

"Tom Griggs," he said.

"Tom, Sam McKall. How are you?"

"Good...fine. How are you?" he said, surprised to be hearing from me.

"Listen, I finished reading over all of the filings you've made with the NRC and I've got a couple of questions. Mind if I stop by on my way home?" I said.

"Well, I'm meeting some people for dinner at the New Yorker. I was just about to leave—"

"The New Yorker? Good, I'll meet you there and we can have a drink at the bar before your dinner. This will only take a minute," I said and hung up the phone before he had a chance to decline.

TWENTY MINUTES LATER I was sitting at the bar in the New Yorker with a club soda, when Tom Griggs walked in smartly dressed in another dark blue suit, complete with a starched white shirt and cuff links.

"Sam, it's nice to see you," he said as he took the seat beside me. "Maker's Mark, neat," he said to the bartender who placed a napkin in front of him and went about pouring the drink.

"Thanks for coming, Tom," I said.

"I'm just flattered you'd meet with me. After that meeting with your boss, I wasn't sure what to expect next. But our offer still stands," he said.

"It's probably nothing. But if I'm reading your NRC filings and the lease between the Consortium and the Pishutes correctly, you have leased 844 acres less than the amount of acreage required by the proposal. Am I missing something?" I said.

The shock was evident on his face but hard to read.

Was he shocked that I had discovered the discrepancy or was it something else? I couldn't really tell.

He made a quick recovery while taking a sip of his drink and then said, "All the land for the project is on the Pishute Reservation. But they don't own it all. We have a separate lease for the 844 acres,"

"Why wasn't it filed with Bureau of Indian Affairs like the other?" I asked.

"Doesn't have to be."

"Why?"

"They don't have jurisdiction," he said, clearly uncomfortable with this line of questioning.

"Who owns the 844 acres?" I asked.

"Don't know the guy's name, but even if I did we aren't required to disclose that to you or anyone else," he said as he took enough cash out of his pocket to cover his drink and a good-sized tip.

"Surely, you don't think you're going to be able to keep something like that a secret," I said.

"Not trying to keep it secret. We're making all the filings and disclosures we are required to make. If and when that becomes relevant or the NRC asks us to disclose we'll do so. Until then it's proprietary. Now if you will excuse me, my dinner guests are waiting," he said and finished his drink.

"Actually, there is just one more question, Tom," I said. He had already taken a couple of steps away from the bar but stopped and looked at me.

"Are you on some kind of win bonus with the Consortium?'

The question hit him like an unexpected blow to the kidney.

"Excuse me?" he said.

"It's a simple question. Are you going to get a bonus from the Consortium if this project is successful?" I was staring into his eyes. He froze for the slightest of seconds while the color drained from his face and then said:

"Good evening, Sam."

"YOU CLEARLY STRUCK some kind of nerve with that last question," Smitty said. We had met at Lucky's to reconnoiter over the day's events.

"That much was clear. What about the tape?" I said.

"The news there is not so good. Tape must have got too hot. Unintelligible from beginning to end. I sent it to the private lab in L.A., to see if they could do anything with it," he said in between bites of meatloaf.

"When will they know something?"

"Won't know until they get it. They'll call me after they receive it tomorrow," he said and held his empty drink glass up so Lucky would see he wanted another.

"That's really disappointing."

My emotions were on such a roller coaster, that the slightest bit of bad news sent me spiraling downward. My experience at the office this afternoon reinforced my fears about how fast the story was getting around. Too many people knew about what was going on. It was only a matter of time before someone in the media picked up on it. If Smitty had not been sitting on the story there is no doubt that it would already be out. Even so, I figured I had two days; three would be an unbelievable stretch.

"You've gotten us three good leads we can work on," Smitty said, sensing that my spirits had fallen with the bad news about the tape. "I don't think I'll have much trouble finding out what Griggs' deal with the Consortium is. Why don't you see if you can find out who our 844-acre man is," he said.

"I was also going to track down Jack Longnight in the morning and see if I can pay him a visit. Want to come?" I said.

"Absolutely. I guess Jack moved up a few places on the mostly likely list," Smitty said, reading my face to see if I had already realized it.

"Wonder what he's making on this deal," he said when I didn't respond.

"Nothing shows up in the documents," I said.

"What? Do you think they got a line item somewhere that says, 'Bride Money for Chief Longnight'."

"He just doesn't seem..." I didn't finish the sentence because I realized how naive it would sound to Smitty.

"Somebody in this thing is crooked," he said a split second before shoving in the last bite of meatloaf.

"I guess I always tend to see the good in people."

"I don't." Smitty was just the opposite; he invariably assumed the worst to be true and required proof to believe otherwise. That was why it was so hard to gain Smitty's respect and so frighteningly easy to lose it.

"That's our plan then," I said to wrap things up.

"Sounds like it."

"Need a ride home?" I said gingerly.

"Naw, I'll have Lucky call me a cab."

"I can wait a while. Got nothing but an empty apartment waiting for me," I said, trying to act as if it were no bother to wait.

"I got some work to do. I'm going to be here a while," he said and patted the top of a manila folder stuffed several inches thick with papers.

"I really don't mind waiting."

"Please Sam. I'm fine," he said in a sharp tone.

"Okay, okay. I am just trying to help," I said.

TO BE HONEST, I have to admit that the moment Calvin Leapingdeer told me about his mother's letter, somewhere in the back of my mind I reluctantly began to suspect that Jack Longnight was involved somehow. But that idea was so foreign to my experience with him that I rejected it without really thinking about it—until Smitty vocalized it at dinner. I reconsidered the circumstances during my drive home, and my suspicions began to grow. When I took personalities out of it, it was even more clear that the evidence was pointing in his direction. The fact that Mary died within hours of revealing her change of heart to Jack was a fairly damning piece of evidence. There was no denying that.

EIGHTEEN

IT WAS A RELIEF when the alarm clock went off the next morning. I was tired of tossing and turning in my bed pretending to sleep. Following my normal morning routine, I made it to my bagel place about 7:00 a.m. Coffee and bagel in hand, I tried to read the papers to kill enough time until I could start making phone calls.

At 8:00 I knew my secretary, Nina, would be in and I could get the phone numbers I needed to begin tracking down Jack Longnight.

"Sam McKall's office, this is Nina," she said, picking up on the first ring.

"Nina, Sam. How are you?"

"Sam. How are you?" she said in a whisper so that no one else in the office would know who she was talking to.

"I'm fine."

"There is a lot of stuff...well, rumors I guess... going around up here," she said.

"What are they saying?" I asked.

"I can't really go into it right now," she said in even a quieter whisper. "But you need to come in here and straighten this out."

"I wish it were that easy, Nina. But it's not. You'll have to trust me that I'm doing the best I can and that it is not true. None of it. No matter what you hear, don't believe it," I said.

"Everybody's talking about it, Sam. What do you want me to say?" she said.

"Nothing. Don't worry about it. It will all work out." I hoped.

"Okay," she said because she was unsure of what else could be said.

"Listen, Nina, I need Jack Longnight's phone numbers. Can you get them for me?" I said.

"Jack Longnight?"

"Yes."

"Certainly, hang on just a sec."

I FOUND JACK at his day job at a hazardous waste dump out near the reservation. He graciously agreed to meet with us but had more than a passing interest in why the Governor's Chief of Staff was bringing a reporter out to meet with him. I offered no explanation.

I collected Smitty from the curb in front of the *Capitol Times* and we headed out toward Utah's West Desert and our meeting with Jack Longnight.

"I think you caught a break on this Valerie Turpin thing," he said after getting in my Jeep.

"Really? What?" I said. I *needed* a break.

"Remember when I was telling you about the phone records and that they still did not have all of them?"

"Yeah, you said they were missing one and they'd be getting it in a day or two."

"That's right, well it took them a little longer than they expected. Call came from out of state, had a hard time getting the phone company to cooperate."

"Where did it come from?" I asked.

"Originated in Maine. Some beach."

"York Beach," I said.

"Yeah, York Beach. That's it. How'd you..." he stopped mid-sentence and looked at me.

"Don't tell me you've been to York Beach, Maine," he said.

"Over Labor Day weekend," I said.

"Call was made from a pay phone at the Union Bluff Hotel the Saturday before Labor Day," he said, referring to a notebook he had produced from his coat pocket.

"Had dinner there that night," I said staring out the front window of my car, numbness beginning to overtake me.

"You have got to be kidding me, Sam," he said. I could feel him staring at me, his jaw slacked.

I just shook my head as I continued to stare at the road in front of me.

"It's not going to take the good ol' Lieutenant James long to figure that out," he said.

"Probably already knows."

"That's more than enough to... I mean I think it's...what do I know. It's all circumstantial," Smitty stammered.

"My guess is that the only reason they haven't is

because I'm Beckstead's Chief. But with this call from Maine—circumstantial or not—its got to be enough,'' I said, trying to make myself face up to what lay ahead.

''They haven't done it yet and that means we've still got time,'' Smitty said.

WE FOUND JACK at his post at the security gate at CleanTech's hazardous waste dump about 15 miles east of the Pishute Reservation. We parked in one of the few stalls in front of the small yellow security building. Jack saw us approaching and opened the gate.

The building was comprised of one office where all incoming and outgoing traffic was logged. Two younger men worked at each of the windows while Jack was working at a small metal desk situated in the middle of the room.

''Come in and have a seat,'' he said as we walked through the door.

''Thank you,'' I said as we each took one of two chairs in front of his desk.

''You see, Sam,'' Jack said, indicating the hazardous waste dump he was guarding, ''what the state has allowed to grow up around our reservation.''

Then turning to Smitty he said, ''It precludes any serious economic development on the reservation, yet when we try to get into the same business, Sam's boss gets very concerned. Interesting isn't it, Wayne.''

''Please, call me Smitty.''

"Why is that, Sam?" Jack said turning his attention back to me.

"I guess he doesn't like the name Wayne," I said, trying to defuse the situation.

"Well it doesn't matter because," Jack said, ignoring my joke, "luckily you don't have any say in what we do on our reservation."

"True enough," I said, ready to change subjects anyway.

"Do you two guys always work together?" he asked.

"Obviously, we don't," I said. "But we have been working on one little project together that I think might interest you."

I waited for Jack to respond, but he just sat there calmly waiting as if he could not possibly care what we had been up to.

"We have been looking into Mary Leapingdeer's death and we found some interesting information," I said.

"The Governor's Chief of Staff and the top political report for the *Times* have teamed up to investigate a bathtub accident?"

"Tell me about the last conversation you had with Ms. Leapingdeer," I said.

"Warm and friendly, like always," he said with a shrug of his shoulders, but a look of concern crept into his eyes.

"And she did not mention that she had planned to change her vote on your nuke dump, Jack?" I said.

His face for the briefest perceptible time showed surprise.

"Mary had always been a supporter of our plans," he said.

"A true statement, but not an answer to my question," I said.

"I'm not sure what you're after," he said, beating a full retreat now.

"Let me make this a little bit simpler for you. Do you know Calvin Leapingdeer?"

"Of course, he's in a prison in New Mexico."

"That's right. Would it surprise you to know that hours before your visit with Mary, she wrote Calvin a letter?" I said and waited for a response from Jack. He sat motionless.

"She told Calvin," I continued, "that she had changed her mind about supporting your project and that she was not looking forward to telling you about it."

"I remember the conversation," he said.

"So you admit it then," I said.

"Admit what?"

"That she told you."

"Of course, I admit it. I've never denied it."

"But you've never told anyone about that conversation either, have you?"

"Yes, of course. I was the last person to see her alive. It's in the police report. Surely, a couple of ace detectives as you and Smitty here have pulled the police report," he said.

I knew I hadn't, so I looked at Smitty.

"Of course we've seen the report, Jack, but that report says nothing about what you and Mary talked about," Smitty said.

"I answered all their questions completely and honestly. They never asked what we talked about so I didn't tell them."

"What did happen at that meeting?" I asked.

"I went out to see Mary early in the afternoon of the day she died. She had called me and asked me to come out. So I did. When I got there she told me that she had reconsidered her position on the facility and that at the next Tribal Council Meeting she was going to bring it up for reconsideration. As I said, it was warm and friendly. Anyone who knew Mary knew it could not have been any other way," he said.

"If it was that harmless, why didn't you tell the police?" I said.

"Like I have already said, Sam, they did not ask. And at the time, it didn't seem unusual that they didn't ask. She slipped and fell in the shower. How could it matter what we talked about?"

"Some people might see that as a motive for murder," Smitty said.

"But she was not murdered. She fell in the shower and hit her head," he said.

"And you appointed her replacement, someone's vote you knew you could count on, and your project was saved," Smitty said.

"I'm sure Sam here can explain to you, Smitty, that it's not a common practice to appoint your enemies to politically sensitive positions. Mary had a very unfortunate accident and as my job requires I appointed her replacement. End of story,'' he said.

''Yet you told no one, not even your own police about the details of your conversation with Mary,'' I said.

''I answered all their questions fully and truthfully. It was an accident. We reported it to the federal authorities. They declined to investigate, because no matter how tragic it was, old ladies slip and fall in the shower every day. Unfortunately, Mary was one of them.'' He was getting a little angry now.

''Then her son, another member of your tribe and opponent of your dump, is killed.''

''In an automobile accident, while he was driving and driving drunk as I understand it,'' he said.

''You don't find that strange?'' I asked.

''No, I don't find it strange and I'll tell you why. Mary's husband—Jeff and Calvin's father—drank himself to death. Calvin is in jail for killing a man while robbing a liquor store. He was drunk at the time. That Jeff was drinking shortly after his mother's death, doesn't surprise me at all. I wish I could say otherwise, but I can't.''

''Why don't we all just calm down a bit,'' Smitty said, holding his hand out as if he were holding something down. ''Jack, I need to be clear on something. You told no one about your conversation with Mary that afternoon?''

Jack's face was placid, but I could see the wheels spinning inside his head. It was obvious that he had told someone and he was trying to decide whether or not he should tell us. Not wanting to let him off the hook, Smitty and I sat perfectly still and quiet.

"When I left," he said finally, "I was on my way to a meeting in Rock Springs. I called Tom Griggs."

"And told him about Mary's change of heart," I said.

"That's right. I thought he'd may as well hear it from me," he said.

"What did he say?" Smitty asked.

"He was concerned. We had always known that Mary was shaky so I don't think he was surprised," Jack said.

"He was mad then," I said.

"Frustrated I would say," Jack said unwilling to let me put words in his mouth.

"Then what?" I said.

"He asked me if I thought I could bring her back around. I told him I didn't know, but that I would try."

"And you were on your way out of town? To Rock Springs?" Smitty said.

"That's right and I have plenty of people who can put me there at the time of the death. If that's what you are getting at," he said.

Smitty and I exchanged an I'm-done-here look.

"Thank you for your time, Jack," I said as we got up to leave.

"Wait a minute," Jack said. "You don't really think somebody killed Mary? Do you?"

"It's looking more and more that way," Smitty said.

"Who?"

"We don't know yet, Jack, but we are getting very close," Smitty said.

NINETEEN

"WHAT DO YOU THINK?" I asked Smitty on the trip back to Wasatch City.

"Let's assume for a minute that his alibi checks out," he said.

"Okay."

"That leaves at least three possible scenarios. One, Jack did it but the coroner got the time of death wrong. Two, coroner's right, but Jack's part of a conspiracy. Three, Jack has nothing to do with it and Tom Griggs or somebody Tom told is responsible," Smitty said.

"What are the chances that the coroner missed the time of death?"

"Not good. I had a medical forensic specialist look at the autopsy report already. He concurred with the time of death. Which of the other two do you like?"

"I guess I lean toward three," I said.

"Why?"

"If he and Griggs had conspired to commit a murder, I don't think he would have even told us about the conversation. He would have simply said he told no one and allowed his alibi to clear him of the murder," I said.

"You're probably right, but one thing to keep in mind is that conspirators often turn on each other as the last act of self-defense. Jack may be feeling us breathing down his neck and is throwing Griggs under the bus," he said.

"Well somebody made the call from the Union Bluff Hotel. And he had to be in Maine to do it," I said.

"When we get back, I'll try to find out who has an alibi for that," Smitty said.

"Meanwhile, Lieutenant James is about two phone calls away from finding out I was in Maine when that phone call was made," I said, sensing that my time was running out very quickly now.

I DROPPED SMITTY at his office and set about to find the 844-acre man. I had no idea how hard it was going to be. After I realized that there was no one in all of state government who could tell me, I called Tracey, who was able to use her connections in the Bureau of Indian Affairs to get me a name: H. Robert Bracken, great grandson to Theodore H. Bracken, one of the West's first railroad barons.

"In the 1880s the federal government was looking at the West Desert as a possible site for the Pishute Indian Reservation," Tracey had said. "Apparently this Theodore H. Bracken was convinced that there was mineable gold and copper out there. So he called in some chits and the government let him maintain an 844-acre in-holding with trespass easements on the reservation. It's the kind of thing you could never get away with now, but this was a century ago when the railroad barons were a powerful political force," she explained.

"I take it they never found the gold and copper," I said.

"Never did. They leased the land to the Defense Department during World War II. I think it was a landing strip or something for training pilots. Anyway, it's been unused since then, not by the Defense Department anyway," Tracey said.

ALTHOUGH THE Bracken family had long since relocated to New York in order to be closer to the nation's financial centers, they were still pretty well known in Utah. In fact, the Governor's Mansion in Wasatch City was originally built by Theodore Bracken around the turn of the century and was purchased by the State when the family left Utah in the 1920s. The Brackens still had a few holdings in Utah, including some prime real estate in downtown Wasatch City, but the Bracken heirs had very little to do with the state where their patriarch had amassed the family's fortune.

All in all, I was left to assume that while they were undoubtedly in it for the money, they didn't need the money and were not likely to be involved in a series of murders to ensure that the project went through.

In short, once again things seemed to be centered on Jack Longnight.

BY THE TIME I had finished my conversation with Tracey, it was late in the evening. I called Smitty and made arrangements to meet him for dinner. At Lucky's of course. I was really beginning to dislike that place.

"Any word on the tape?" I asked, skipping the hello.

"Talked to the guy about an hour ago, nothing yet. But he is optimistic they'll be able to reclaim at least some of it."

"How long?"

"Maybe tomorrow he said. I asked him to rush it for me. But I'm not his biggest client, if you know what I mean."

"It's not hopeless then?"

"He didn't think so. Course guys like that never do."

"Guys like that?"

"Techies, computer geeks."

"It is at least something," I said feeling even less hopeful than I sounded.

"Brought you a copy of the story that's going to run tomorrow," he said, pointing to piece of paper in front of my place at the booth.

I picked it up and began reading:

> Hours before her death last month, Mary Leapingdeer, a respected member of the Pishute Tribal Council, made known her plans to oppose the Tribe's plans to build a nuclear waste dump on its West Desert Reservation.
>
> The *Capitol Times* has learned that on the af-

ternoon of her death Leapingdeer met with Tribal Chief Jack Longnight and told him of her plans to switch her deciding vote from favoring to opposing the controversial multi-billion dollar project.

Hours later the 82-year-old Leapingdeer died in what tribal authorities have determined was an accidental fall in her bathub.

After Leapingdeer's death Longnight appointed Barney Nez to the council. Nez, a longtime political ally of Longnight, strongly supports the Tribe's deal with a consortium of five out-of-state utility companies to build the nuclear waste dump. His appointment secured the project's support on the council.

When the project was first announced, Leapingdeer, citing the desperate need for economic development on the Pishute Indian Reservation, supported the project.

But Leapingdeer's son, Jeff Leapingdeer, an attorney for World Resources Defense Council, an environmental advocacy group, was eventually able to persuade his mother that the project was not in the Pishute's best interest.

When asked why he had never disclosed the nature of his last conversation with Leapingdeer, Longnight said that, "No one asked me and it didn't seem relevant."

The project proposal, which was first made public six months ago, is currently awaiting the approval of the Nuclear Regulatory Commission.

Jeff Leapingdeer died within days of his mother's death in a tragic one-car accident near his home in San Francisco.

"Jack should enjoy reading that over his morning coffee," I said.

"Hey, I was a lot more gentle with him than I had to be," Smitty said. And he was right. There was only the slightest hint that Mary may have been murdered to keep her from changing her vote. But for those who picked up on that hint, as Jack certainly would, the implication was clear.

"Hopefully, it's enough to break something loose for us," I said. "We need a break."

"Started checking alibis after I filed the story," Smitty said.

"And?"

"Jack's Rock Springs alibi checks out air tight, and the same for Labor Day Weekend. Tom Griggs was in Duluth, Minnesota with his family. It all checks out."

"Both of them?" I said.

"Yeah, both of them. Someone else made that call," he said.

"But who?" I said, racking my own brain.

"That I can't tell you. What did you find out about the 844-acre man?"

"Yet another dead end, I'm afraid. It's owned by the Bracken family." I went into a play-by-play on how I had learned about the Bracken family's involvement with the land in question.

"Well I doubt what's left of the Bracken clan could find its way out to Utah even if they did want to kill somebody," Smitty said with a chuckle. "Although, they say Ted IV is a mean bastard."

"We don't even have that going for us. Apparently, this little piece of the Bracken empire is owned by Robert Bracken," I explained.

"H. Robert Bracken?" he asked with heightened interest.

"H. Robert, that's right. Why?"

"Back in the late '70s early '80s, one of the Brackens, I believe it was H. Robert, was convicted of mail fraud. I can't remember the details. But as I recall, H. Robert and Ted IV got in quite a power struggle over who was going to control the Bracken Family Trust when Ted III died. H. Robert got caught with his hand in the cookie jar and went to a federal country club for about 2 years. While he was in, Ted IV basically cut him off from any of the family money. From what I hear H. Robert is able to keep up appearances but struggles financially. Ted IV gives him just enough to keep him out of the unemployment line," Smitty said.

"How did he end up with the 844 acres?" I wondered out loud.

"Could have just fallen through the cracks. Could have figured it was worthless and just let him keep it. Could have been Ted IV's idea of a joke," Smitty said.

"Maybe it's not such a dead end after all," I said. "I'm going back to the office and search the archives and see what I can come up with on Mister H. Robert Bracken,'' Smitty said and finished his freshly served scotch in one big gulp.

''Should I call you when I'm done?'' he said after slamming the tumbler down on the table.

''Absolutely.''

''Probably going to be late.''

''Won't bother me. It'll give me something to do besides stare at the ceiling in my bedroom.''

When the elevator opened on the hall that led to my apartment, it was crowded with policemen. I was caught off guard for a second before I realized that all the activity was centered on my apartment.

''What's going on here?'' I asked from my doorway as uniformed and plain-clothes cops rifled through my belongings.

''He's here, Fred,'' one of them yelled without taking particular notice of me.

A moment later Lt. Fred James walked through my bedroom door with a wicked smile. It struck me how much that smile needed to be knocked off his face.

''Mister McKall, I thought we might meet again,'' he said, shoving a piece of paper in my face.

''What are you—''

''Mr. McKall, that is a duly signed warrant to search these premises. If you would like to stay you will have to be quiet, stay out of our way, and not interfere with our search,'' he said, enjoying himself entirely too much.

I assumed that they had discovered my whereabouts on Labor Day weekend and this search was just a prelude to an arrest. I tried not to let the fear show on my face, but I knew James could read it all over me.

"I've nothing to hide, you could have searched my place anytime you wanted without this," I said holding up his warrant.

"We like it better this way. Less questions later," he said.

"Take your time," I said, noticing that the warrant was accentuating the nervous shaking in my hands.

"We will, Mister McKall," he said as he headed back toward my bedroom.

I positioned myself so that I could see what was going on in my laundry room. There was a female officer, somewhere in her twenties, methodically searching through my dirty clothes. I tried not to stare at her, but occasionally glanced over to see what she was doing.

After she finished the clothes, she started on the shelves, box after box, can after can, bucket after bucket. She searched everything on the shelves. Next she turned her attention to the items on top of my dryer.

There she was, a matter of inches away from the most incriminating evidence that had thus far been manufactured. I felt somewhat like Dostoyevsky's Raskolnikov when he was confronted by the police. My heart raced, pounding so loud in my chest that its noise drowned everything else. My eyes focused on the box of laundry detergent where I had hidden the key.

I felt a bead of sweat run down my forehead as she reached for the box soap. I was almost in a full-scale panic when she noticed me staring at the box. My eyes lifted from the box to hers. Our eyes locked for a long moment, before I managed to tear myself away and give the pretence of having only a passing interest in her search.

I tried to keep track of what she was doing using only my peripheral vision. But it was impossible to observe her in enough detail to tell what she was doing. After a long, terrifying moment she walked from the laundry room into the kitchen.

As casually as I could, I glanced into the laundry room. The box of soap was gone.

I'm not sure what the police did after that. I stumbled to one of the chairs at my kitchen table and sat down. I just sat there staring at my hands while the officers finished their search.

About 10:00 p.m. they left en masse, taking all the nuclear documents I had copied and four, maybe five other boxes full of my things, including the box of soap.

I figured it would take no more than 24 hours to find the key, trace it to the bus station and find the gym bag. And I would be in jail with a mountain of evidence piled up against me.

I CLOSED AND LOCKED my door after the last policeman had left and made a beeline for the laundry room. I found what I was afraid of, the officer had in fact, taken the box of laundry soap. I was reasonably sure however, that she only took it because she saw me staring at it and that it would not be immediately clear why I was interested in that box of soap. Although once they started looking, it would not take them long to find the key.

As I worried over my stupidity, the phone rang. I answered it and found Smitty on the other end.

"You'll never guess what just happened here," I said.

"I bet I can. The police just showed up with a search warrant."

"How'd you know?"

"Just a guess. They find the key to the bus locker?"

"One of the officers caught me staring at the detergent box I hid it in and she took it. I don't think they know what they have yet. She just took it because I was looking at it," I said, feeling very stupid.

"Try not to worry about that. We've got to concentrate on our own investigation, we are almost out of time. Now I've pulled together all the information in our archives about Mr. H. Robert Bracken and his family struggles. You want to see it?"

"Absolutely."

"Want me to come over there?"

"Sounds good. See you in ten."

AT 10:30 SMITTY and I were sitting at my kitchen table passing photocopied news stories back and forth as we each read the sordid details of H. Robert Bracken Jr.'s life.

To say that a Bracken child was born with a silver spoon in his mouth was to say Babe Ruth was an adequate center fielder with a pretty good stick. Born in 1947, H. Robert had every advantage a child has ever had. His parents had weathered the Great Depression by dividing their time between Park Avenue, the Hamptons and West Palm Beach. What little of their time remained after the busy social calendar was divided among their three children, Theodore H. IV, H. Robert and Eliza. Eliza had been the oldest child but had succumbed to polio in her early teens, when Robert was but an infant.

Theodore and Robert followed parallel tracks throughout their childhood and adolescent years. The finest nannies, the finest prep schools, world travel and of course Ivy League educations. But this is where Robert and Theodore began parting ways. Theodore, the oldest son enrolled in Princeton, while Robert, two years the junior, matriculated at Brown.

During Robert's sophomore year at Brown, his father and mother died in a plane crash 250 miles north of West Palm. Two months later Robert dropped out of Brown and as far as I could tell never darkened the door of any university again. Theodore, who was now clearly shaping up to be the good son, finished his finance degree and moved on to Harvard for his MBA.

In what appeared to be a mutually agreeable situation, Theodore looked after the family's money, while Robert played. Even though neither his father nor grandfather had ever worked a day in their lives,

Theodore IV seemed driven to make his own name in the business world. Theodore IV, it appeared, had inherited his great-grandfather's steely eyes and Midas touch. The Bracken trust began to grow by leaps and bounds as he risked his family's fortune in high stakes real-estate ventures and traditional manufacturing concerns. Before long, Theodore IV was the toast of Wall Street.

His brother Robert, on the other hand, had moved to Europe, living there between 1965-1972. In 1972, after moving back to the family's Park Avenue apartment, he met and married a New York socialite cut from much the same cloth as himself. It must have been about that time, Smitty speculated, that Theodore must have gotten tired of supporting Robert's extravagant lifestyle and demanded he at least pretend to earn his keep. But whatever the reason, in 1975, Robert accepted a position with Bracken International Inc., and this seems to be where the real friction between the brothers began.

Bracken International was Theodore's baby. He controlled its activities from top to bottom, inside to out. Robert was given a nice title of Executive Vice-President but was squarely under his brother's thumb. His career at Bracken International lasted all of 18 months.

Next stop for Robert was his wife's father's company, Standard Manufacturing Ltd. This is where Robert ran afoul of the law. He had been working at Standard for almost three years when he was arrested, for fraud and embezzlement. After a year's long legal battle with the Department of Justice, he was able to plead the charges down to simple wire fraud and was sentenced to 2 years in a minimum-security prison. His wife, of course, had long since left him by the time he was parolled in 1981 which left him with only one option—throw himself on his brother's mercy.

Theodore provided Robert with the bare neccessities: a Park Avenue apartment and a six-figure allowance. It was enough, just barely, for Robert to maintain appearances of the idle rich but not nearly enough to keep him in the style to which he had grown accustomed.

"THAT'S IT, that's all we got on the guy," Smitty said after we had both finished reading the news stories.

"H. Robert lookes like a guy who might want this dump to go through as bad as anybody," I said.

"If he's making anything like the Pishutes are making on their lease, it could be worth hundreds of millions over the life of the lease," Smitty said. I was willing to bet that he had driven even a harder bargain than Jack, but still $100 million would put H. Robert right back in his old rich and famous lifestyle jetting between New York and the South of France.

"Any idea how to get hold of this guy?" I asked.

"I'm on it at 8:00 East Coast Time tomorrow morning," Smitty said.

"I'm likely to be in jail that time tomorrow you realize," I said as he began to gather up his newspaper stories.

"We got it narrowed down to Tom Griggs, Jack

Longnight and H. Robert. Maybe something will break when we find H. Robert.''

''I certainly hope so.''

SMITTY LEFT AROUND 1:00 a.m., and I found enough to do that I did not have to lay down until about 2:30 a.m. Sleep did not come easily. I lay bright-eyed staring at the ceiling and wondering what tomorrow would bring.

TWENTY

I WAS AWAKE when my alarm clock went off at 5:30. Smitty had said he would begin tracking down H. Robert at 6:00 a.m. Utah Time, 8:00 a.m. East Coast Time. I figured I could call him about 6:30, so I had an hour to kill fiddling around the apartment.

At 6:30 sharp I called Smitty, but got his voice mail. I decided he must be on the phone. I called every ten minutes until 7:30 before I decided to leave a message. Another agonizing hour went by before I decided to call the main number to the News Room.

"Is Smitty in?" I asked the man who answered the phone.

"No, he's not, can I put you through to his voice mail?"

"No, I've already left him a message there. Do you know what time to expect him?"

"Mr. Smith was in a automobile accident last night. I don't think he will be in today."

"Is he alright?"

"Honestly, I don't know his condition. He's at University Hospital."

"Thank you," I said after I had already started hanging up the phone.

In one motion I dropped my coffee mug, grabbed my car keys and ran out of my apartment.

I FOUND SMITTY asleep in a private room. There were bandages on his head and stitches scattered over his face. Leaving his room I found a nurse stationed at a desk not far down the hall.

"How is Mr. Smith?" I asked.

"He's going to be fine. He had a pretty nasty blow to the head, and a compound fracture of the fibula," the fortysomething nurse said.

"How did it happen?" I asked.

"I'm sorry, I don't know."

"What time was he brought in?"

She picked up a chart and looked through its pages. "About 2:00 a.m.," she said.

"How can I find out what happened?" I asked.

"Call this number at the Wasatch County Sheriff's office. They brought him in," she said and handed me a pre-printed slip of paper with a phone number on it. In my hurry to leave my house I had left my cell phone, so I found the nearest pay phone and dialed the number.

"Accident Reports, Susan," a very pleasant voice said.

"I'm calling about an accident last night, involving Wayne Smith," I said.

"Yes. We've had several calls. What can I do for you?"

"Can you tell me what happened?"

"It was a one-car accident on Wasatch Boulevard

and about 7800 South. Time of accident 01:15 hours.''

''What was the cause of the accident?''

''Undetermined at this time. Mr. Smith was unconscious when officers arrived on the scene.''

''Was alcohol involved?''

''Given Mr. Smith's record, we have ordered a blood test from the hospital, but we haven't received the results yet.''

''Thank you,'' I said and hung up the phone. I wasn't sure what to think. He had left my apartment less than an hour before the accident. And even though I could smell alcohol on his breath, he didn't seem drunk to me. In fact, just the opposite seemed true, he was as sharp and cogent as always. Yet, I was beginning to understand that Smitty did have a drinking problem, and despite everything that was going on I couldn't rule out the idea that he could have been drunk and that this accident was caused by nothing more than that. Although it did seem unlikely.

I walked back to the nurses' station where the same nurse was still working at a computer.

''Has Mr. Smith been conscious since being admitted?'' I asked.

''Oh yes. I think he came to in the ambulance on the way over. He is on some pretty strong pain medication for his leg. That's why he's asleep. He's scheduled in the OR this afternoon,'' she said.

''Has the blood alcohol test come back?''

''Oh, I can't release that information. I'm sorry,''

she said as if she were mildly offended at my question.

"No problem. Has his family been notified?"

"He said not to. He gave us the name of Sam McKall, but I haven't been able to reach him yet this morning."

"I'm Sam McKall. Was there any message?" I said.

"No message, he just gave us your name and number and asked that we notify you," she said with a warm smile, less concerned about me now.

"I'm going to be down here using this pay phone. Will you let me know when he wakes up?" I asked.

"Gladly."

I DIDN'T WANT to leave Smitty, but with the police breathing down my neck, I had to be about the business of finding H. Robert, so I decided to set up office on the pay phone.

Using my calling card, I began by finding numbers for Bracken International. It took me no less than four separate calls and ten transfers to get to Ted IV's receptionist, who, after some persuasion, was able to give me a home number for Robert.

His home number was answered by an answering service who refused to give out any information on his whereabouts, saying only that he was out of town, but checking in twice daily for messages.

"Okay then, ask him to call me please. Sam McKall, with Utah Governor Beckstead," I said and left him the number that rings directly to my desk.

Next I called Jack Longnight. I found him working at CleanTech.

"Jack, I need to get in touch with Robert Bracken. Do you know how I can reach him?"

"He lives in New York," Jack said.

"Yes, but how can I get in touch with him?"

"How would I know? I've never spoken with the man."

"During all your negotiations with the Consortium, you've never had an occasion to talk to Robert Bracken?" I said, the incredulity dripping from my voice.

"No, as a matter of fact I didn't. Tom Griggs handled all of that," Jack said.

"Do you have Tom's number handy? I'm not at my office," I said.

"I can't believe Smitty doesn't have it," he said as he shuffled through some papers on his desk.

"Smitty is in the hospital," I said.

"Oh?" Jack said.

"Car accident, late last night."

"Was he drinking and driving again?" Jack said.

"I don't know the details, Jack. Do you have the number?" I said, my patience wearing thin.

"I've got it right here, keep your pants on," he said and gave me the number.

My next call was to Tom.

"What can I help you with, Sam?" Tom said coldly.

"I need to get in touch with Robert Bracken," I said.

"Why?"

"Why did you lie about not remembering when I asked you about him the other night?" I said.

"His name slipped my mind. What's the big deal?"

"That's not what you said. You said you couldn't remember who owned the land. You remembered, you just didn't want to tell me. Why?"

"It's none of your business who we do business with. That's why."

"You guys don't mind answering any of the other questions we have, why lie about Bracken?" I said.

"Sam, I don't have time to argue with you. Here's Bracken's number," he said and gave me the number I had already.

"Not that number, you know he's not in New York. I need to contact him right now. Where is he today?"

"I don't know where he is day to day," he said.

"Is he in town?" I asked.

"I...I don't know where he is. When I want to talk to him I call the number I just gave you and leave a message. He always gets right back to me."

"Where does he stay when he's in town?" I said, sure that he was still lying.

"I don't know where he stays. He's a grown man, he stays where he wants," he said.

Looking down the hall, I saw the nurse approaching. When she noticed I was looking at her, she stopped and pointed at Smitty's door to let me know he was awake.

"Tell him I'm looking for him," I said, hung up and ran down to Smitty's room.

When I walked in Smitty was awake but groggy.

"Sammy, you made it," he whispered through dry cracked lips.

"How are you?" I asked as I approached the bed.

"Beat to hell," he said, straining under the pain of talking. His face, what part of it that was not bandaged, was red and swollen, and his arms which had been tucked under the blankets when I first saw him, were scratched and bruised.

"How's your leg?"

"Worse."

"What happened?" I asked.

"I was driving home on Wasatch Boulevard," his speech was slurred and barely audible with long gaps between words. "Right after it merges down to a two-lane road... Car came zooming up behind me... Tried to pass me on the curve... I swerved to miss him and lost control... The next thing I remember is waking up in an ambulance."

"Were you drinking?"

"You saw me, Sam, I wasn't drunk," he said.

"I saw you the night you were busted for a DUI and you didn't seem drunk to me then either," I said.

There was an awkward silence.

"Yes, I was drinking."

"After you left my apartment?"

"I took a sip in the garage...from my flask."

"A sip?"

"Okay, more than a sip," he said. "But I wasn't drunk, Sammy."

"Well they've done a blood test. I don't know the results, but they did one. And if you were drunk, I may be the only person in this world willing to believe that someone ran you off that road."

"I'll just have to live with that," he said.

"I've been trying to get in touch with Robert Bracken ever since I found out you were in here, with no luck at all. Do you have any suggestions?" I said after a moment.

"Tell me what you have done so far," he said. And I did.

"If he's behind all this, either Jack Longnight or Tom Griggs knows about it or are in on it with him. They'll get him the message. I don't think you need to worry. If it's him, he'll find you," Smitty said, his eyes beginning to close under the effects of the medication.

"Before the police do I hope," I said as he faded away.

TWENTY-ONE

BEST CASE SCENARIO, I had the remainder of the day. Surely, finding Valerie's gym bag would be enough to remove what little doubts Lt. James and his superiors might have. Though I desperately racked my brain for a lead to pursue something with the few hours that remained of my freedom, I could come up with nothing. I had tried everything I knew. Everything was a dead end.

Smitty was back asleep and no use to me now as he lay in a hospital bed. Dejected, I left the room and went down the hall to the pay phone to check my messages to see if Robert Bracken had returned my call.

The only message was from Tracey who had received the inevitable call.

''Sam, I got a call from a Lieutenant Fred James this morning. I've got to talk to you about it before I call him back. I'm sure it is about this mess in Wasatch City,'' her message said.

The whole thing had been so depressing I had not even called her to tell her about the threatening call from the Union Bluff Hotel. I regretted that now.

"Tracey. How are you?" I asked after I got her on the phone.

"I'm fine. The question is how are you?"

"Things are not looking good. Smitty was in an accident last night. He's laid up in the hospital."

"How is he?"

"I haven't talked to his doctor, but his leg is broken pretty bad and he got banged up pretty good."

"Was he drinking?"

"Yeah, but he says he was run off the road. Police are calling it a one-car accident and have ordered a blood test."

"What do you think?"

"He was with me less than an hour before it happened, seemed sober to me."

"So what do you think? Was he run off the road?"

"Could be, I don't know."

"It's all so frightening," she said. "Listen, I got a call this morning from a Lieutenant James on the Wasatch PD. Do you know what it's about?"

"Yeah, unfortunately I do. There was another threatening phone call to Valerie Turpin over Labor Day weekend." I paused as I tried to think of how best to continue.

"So why are they calling me?"

"They traced the call, and it appears that the call came from the Union Bluff Hotel the night we were having dinner there with your family."

"What?"

"That's right. Somebody must have followed us there and called from a pay phone while we were having dinner. I'm sure they're calling to confirm what time we were there."

"In the hotel? While we were eating?" she said.

"That's right," I said and realized for the first time that if I was having trouble believing Smitty's story, it would be completely understandable if Tracey were having a hard time believing mine.

There was silence while I waited on her to respond. To say something. Anything. I felt as if my whole life hung on here next word.

"It's all so..." she said, searching for the right word.

"Unbelievable," I offered, fearing the worst.

"Well, yes, it is unbelievable, but the word I was looking for is...misconstrued," she finally landed on it.

"Misconstrued?" I said, somewhat relieved.

"Yes, whoever is doing this to you is incredibly lucky," she said.

"How so?"

"Okay, if I remember correctly, you told me that the stalking of Valerie began before you and Smitty, or at least you began looking to the Leapingdeers' deaths."

"That's right."

"Yet the whole thing has been set up in such a way that the moment you begin poking around they simply add one more twist and construe things to look as though you had been doing it all along. I mean without a bad guy to focus on who knows where the police investigation would have gone. They never would have made the connection between some perverted calls and an after-hours office break into Senator Voss's file."

"No, they never would have missed that file if I had not asked her about it," I offered.

"See what I mean. Lucky."

"Un-lucky, really. If I didn't ask about that file they'd just make a few more nasty calls and let the whole thing die. No one would ever be the wiser. Valerie might never have even missed that file."

"Yes, but the frightening thing is that the whole thing was constructed anticipating a problem like the one you created for them. But in their wildest dreams they could not have hoped for someone like you to fall into their laps," she said.

"Like me?"

"Yes, you. You are acquainted with the victim. You work together occasionally, but not often. Just close enough for you to develop an obsession from afar, so to speak. I don't know what the profile of a typical stalker is, but I bet that's pretty typical. And just in case being a stalker didn't fit, you came with your own motive."

"What?" I could not believe what I was hearing.

"I'm sorry, that sounded worse than I meant it. I'm just saying that you did not want Voss to succeed politically. The Voss versus Beckstead feud is well documented. Just look at it, you showed up with your own motive, just in case theirs doesn't work. They may think you concocted this whole stalker front to cover your real motive. It is a perfect misconstruction," she said.

"That is why this call from Maine is so damning," I said. "It removes what little reasonable doubt was left. It is the coup de grace. I'll probably be in jail by tonight."

"Jail?" she said.

"Yes, jail. You just said it yourself, airtight case."

"You think they are going to arrest you?"

"If I wasn't Beckstead's chief and they weren't concerned about making a mistake, I'd be in jail right now."

"I can't believe it," she said.

"They executed a search warrant at my apartment last night," I said, deciding not to tell her about the gym bag.

"You've got to be kidding me, Sam. They searched your apartment?"

"I can literally feel the noose tightening around my neck," I said.

"I had no idea it had gotten this far," she said. I guess I had done a good job of playing it down.

"Things have happened fast," I said, exhaling. I was actually feeling a little better now that Tracey seemed to understand what was happening to me.

"What can I do?" she asked. And I was tempted to put her to work helping me find Robert Bracken. But I thought better of it.

"Look, there's not that much you can do at this point and besides I am afraid that if you get involved they'll find some way to come after you as well. These people are nothing if not resourceful.''

''Who's behind it all? Do you have any idea?'' she said.

''Well, we narrowed it down to Jack Longnight or Tom Griggs, who you know, and H. Robert Bracken,'' I said.

''Jack Longnight?''

''He had a motive and he was the last person to see Mary alive,'' I said.

''Motive? I thought he and Mary were on the same side,'' she said.

''Mary changed her mind only hours before her death. She wrote her son Calvin that she was worried about having to tell Jack,'' I explained.

''This Bracken guy,'' she said. ''He's the one I dug up for you, one of the railroad Brackens?''

''They've been out of the railroad business for half a century, but yes, he's one of those Brackens,'' I explained.

''Correct me if I'm wrong, Sam, but those people sold their interest in the railroad and left Utah, taking with them about half of the state's net worth. Why would they even care about this deal?''

''They wouldn't. H. Robert Bracken is a different matter. He's sort of the black sheep of the family. His brother Theodore controls the family fortune and he has all but cut Robert off. Some how this 844-acre plot of land smack dab in the middle of the Pishute Reservation has remained in Robert's name. He's the mystery man in all this. We haven't so much as spoken to him. Can't track him down," I explained.

"And Tom Griggs?"

"Don't really have much on him. Just that he could have a large bonus riding on the success of the project, and Jack Longnight called him after his meeting with Mary," I said.

"It doesn't take much to get on your suspect list," Tracey said.

"I know, but it is all we've been able to come up with and I'm running out of time."

"Are you sure there is nothing I can do?" she asked.

"Just keep believing in me. It looks more and more like that's all I've got going for me."

AFTER TALKING TO Tracey I walked back down and checked on Smitty, who was sound asleep. Returning to my post at the pay phones, I tried Bracken's service again and left another message. Just to let him know that I was not going to give up.

Then I called the newsroom at the *Capitol Times*. It took me thirty minutes before I could find someone who could tell me where Smitty had sent Jeff Leapingdeer's tape. Once I had them on the phone, it took another ten minutes to find the technician who was working on it.

"We've got some of it back," the technician said after I had convinced him it was alright to tell me what was going on with the tape.

"How much?" I said.

"Not much I'm afraid. Only about 12 seconds," he said. "Want to hear it?"

"Yeah," I said.

"Okay hold on and I'll cue it up," he said.

"Here's what I got," he said.

Then came a loud hissing sound like that of a tape recorder, only amplified several times.

"...it needs to go out by the end of the day. Put Wayne Smith on my call list for tomorrow. Send some flowers and a thank you card to..." the hissing stopped.

"That's all I've got so far," he said.

"How long before you're done with the rest of it?"

"Well, like I told Smitty, I can't reclaim some of this. Least not with the equipment we've got here. What I can reclaim should be done...oh I don't know, this time tomorrow," he said.

"Anything we can do to speed that up?" I asked.

"No. I'm doing it as fast as I can, but it's slow and I've only got so much time on the computer. I've already gone over the budget that Smitty gave me."

"Don't stop, keep going. The money's not going to be a problem. I promise," I said.

"That's what I figured," he said.

"Smitty or I will call tomorrow. In the meantime if you reclaim anything about a nuclear project, a meeting he was going to that night or a company by the name of Waste Solutions, call me immediately. If you get my voice mail, play the tape on your message," I said and gave him my home number.

"No problem, glad to."

WEATHER WISE, it was a perfect day, sunny and warm with the slightest hint of a breeze. It was 2:00 in the afternoon and I felt like I had wasted my day, although I could not think of another thing I could have done with it. The sense of dread and panic that had been gradually building ever since Bill Nelson had brought Lt. James in to see me was building rapidly now to a crescendo. And now with the police investigation closing in around me, a sense of helplessness began to grow as well.

It seemed all there was to do was to wait. Wait for the police. I was too preoccupied to read or work. My mind would not be diverted. Around my apartment I paced all afternoon, never stopping. Random thoughts about the conspiracy flew in and out of my mind so fast that I could not focus on any of them. The faster they came, the faster I paced. Back and forth, from the kitchen to the bedroom, from the bedroom to the living room and then back again. Over and over, stopping only to check my messages at the office every few minutes and to leave several more messages with Bracken's service.

About 8:00 p.m. I realized I had not eaten anything all day and decided to go out for a bite, hoping the diversion would calm my mind.

AS I WALKED out of my apartment building and into the parking lot, a dark blue car, a Buick maybe, parked at the far end of the lot turned on its lights and pulled up so that it was between my car and me.

I was standing by the passenger side window. The window was rolled down.

I bent down to look into the car. The driver was a man in his late '50s. I recognized the face, but could not place it.

"My office says you've been looking for me, Mister McKall," the man said. His face was long and slender with bushy eyebrows.

"Do I know you?" I said as I extended my hand in an offer to shake hands.

"You think you do. Why don't you get in," he said.

I was about to refuse when in a deliberate fashion he looked down to his lap, where a sport coat was spread over his legs. From under the coat, he pulled his left hand just far enough that I could see that he was aiming a gun at me. At that moment, I recognized his face.

"H. Robert Bracken," I said, backing away from the car.

"Get in the car, Mister McKall," he said, raising his voice. The photos in the news clippings Smitty had showed me the night before were at least 15 years old and photocopied, but it was definitely him.

I hesitated for a moment, considering my options. There was no cover nearby and even if he were just a reasonable shot I could not get far enough away from him fast enough to avoid being hit.

I opened the passenger side door and got in.

"Put these on," he said and threw a pair of handcuffs in my lap.

I stared at him, then at the cuffs, then back at him.

"Now, Mister McKall," he said as he cocked the gun.

Seeing I had no choice but compliance, I put the cuffs on one wrist and was about to apply the second cuff when he said:

"Through that handle first," indicating that he wanted me to string the cuffs through the handle on the car door before putting them on my other wrist. Shaking my head in disbelief, I did as I was told. Once the cuffs were on he reached over and checked that I had done it properly, tightening each cuff so that they were cutting off the blood circulation in my hands. Then putting the gun back in his lap, he put the car into gear and drove off.

"You're very persistent, Mister McKall. Was it worth it?" He spoke with the hint of a British accent.

"We have the tape," I said, thinking it may save my life.

"Jeff Leapingdeer's tape?" he said with a sneer. "There's nothing on that tape. It's not going to save you."

"You can't be certain of that," I said.

"Leapingdeer never knew about me. He was called to a meeting about the project. No names were ever mentioned. I assure you whatever is on that tape cannot implement me in anything," he said.

"Once you kill your fall guy," I said referring to myself, "they won't have me to blame anymore. They'll be looking for my murderer instead."

"Do you think I've come this far, done this much,

just to foolishly place a gun to your head and pull the trigger. I admit that it would give me great satisfaction to do so. But alas, Mister McKall, I am not that stupid,'' he said with a bile-tainted laugh.

Moments later he turned onto I Street. Though I had never been there I remembered from my interrogation by Lt. James that this was the street on which Valerie Turpin lived.

''Come on, Bracken,'' I pleaded. ''This is between you and me, leave Valerie out of this. She's got nothing to do with this.''

''I wish I could, Mister McKall. But you and that...that reporter would not let it go. You couldn't just let it go. An old lady had an accident in the shower. Why couldn't everybody just let it be. She was 88. Happens all the time,'' he said more to himself than me as he pulled over to the curb and parked.

''Please, Bracken, not Valerie. She doesn't have anything to do with this. I am begging you don't do it.''

''Your wrong, ol' boy. Without her there is no closure. And that's what is needed, closure.''

''This isn't going to bring closure. Think about it,'' I said.

''No, Mister McKall, you think about it, more often than not, how do these stalking incidents end? The old murder/suicide. There's one on the news practically every day. And you've been stalking this poor girl for so long now, done so many horrible things to her, that although people will be shocked by it all, they won't really be surprised,'' he said, his mood actually lightening as he thought about his plan.

''Smitty will know the truth,'' I said and wished I hadn't the moment I did.

''That drunk? Alcohol will be the death of him. Soon, very soon. I just hope he doesn't take an innocent with him. The way you did,'' he said with mocking sadness.

Without another word he leaned over to my side of the car and opened the glove box and removed a coil of rope. As he did he inadvertently rustled some papers under which I thought I saw the very tip of a gun barrel. He quickly shut the glove box, while I pretended to be looking at my handcuffs.

He put on the coat that had been laying in his lap and put his gun in one pocket and the rope in the other.

''I'll be back for you momentarily,'' he said and got out of the car. I watched him very carefully as he walked around to the rear of the house three doors down on the opposite side of the street.

As soon as he was out of sight I began working on the handle through which my handcuffs were locked. Turning so that my two hands were between my feet and my feet were on the door I began to kick and pull the handle simultaneously. The cuffs, which were already cutting off the circulation, began digging into my wrist even deeper. But I continued to kick and pull with all my strength.

I began to worry that it was taking too long and redoubled my efforts. Finally there was a snap somewhere inside the door. I heard it very clearly, it was a loud plastic snap. The handle suddenly loosened. Viciously, I began pulling and kicking harder and faster. Gradually the entire door panel began to loosen until it eventually came off entirely. Although my cuffs were still interlaced through the handle, the handle and its panel were now free from the door.

Completely out of breath, but nevertheless feeling the effects of an incredible adrenaline rush, I reached over and reopened the glove box. And just as I thought I had seen, there was a gun. I checked the clip and was relieved to see that it was loaded.

My door would not open, so I slid over and opened the driver's side door. With some difficulty I got out, pulling the door panel around the steering wheel.

The door panel banged heavily against my knees as it dangled on the chain between the handcuffs. But, holding the gun in one hand and trying to hold the panel with my other, I was able to make pretty good time.

Valerie's house, like most on I Street was old and small but not without a certain charm, which completely escaped me as I made my way up the driveway and to the back door.

It was open.

Carefully I stepped into the house. The rear entry doubled as a laundry room and as such was very crowded. I was being extra careful not to bang the door panel against anything that would make noise. My hands were cold and beginning to feel the numbness caused by the lack of circulation. The weight of the panel pulling against the cuff was making matters much worse.

The house was dark inside, the only light provided by a street lamp shining through the front window. I stood still and listened. Nothing. Not a sound. The house was perfectly quiet and still. I worried that I was too late.

Carefully, I moved further into the house. Next to the laundry was a small cramped little kitchen. There were a few dirty dishes on a small table. The need to be quiet and the unwieldy way I had to carry the door panel made my progress through the house frustratingly slow.

From the kitchen, I made my way into a living room, furnished only with a sofa and two wooden chairs. From the living room I could see a hallway, also dark, except for a shut door, with a dim light emanating from the space between it and the floor.

Cautiously, I made my way over to the door and opened it. In front of me was a stairway, dimly lit by a light on in a basement room. Still not a sound. Nothing. Just silence.

Delicately, I stepped on to the first stair. I waited for a squeak but none came. Then the second. Third. As I reached the fourth, I heard the crying. It was a muffled cry. Quietly but quickly I finished descending the stairs. At the bottom there was a narrow hallway leading back the opposite direction of the stairs, at the end of the hallway, in the direction of the crying was a door. The crying was louder now and more pitiful. It was the crying of fear.

Cautiously and quietly I approached the door and slowly peeked in. The first thing I saw was a bedpost. Then a hand lashed to it. An arm trembling. Bracken was staring at me but holding the gun to Valerie's forehead, each of her limbs lashed to a bed post.

WHEN SHE SAW ME, the fear in her eyes rose another twisted level. The crying took on the tone of a complete emotional breakdown.

"Put down the gun, Bracken. It's over," I said. Unable to aim the gun and hold the panel, it dangled between my hands on the handcuff chain. It took all my strength to hold the gun steady against the swaying of the panel.

Bracken said nothing. Just stared at me and continued holding the gun to her head.

"I mean it, Bracken, I'll do it," I said, my hands starting to tremble.

Still he stared without a word.

I cocked my gun and took a few more steps into the room.

"NOW, BRACKEN," I yelled but startled only Valerie.

Slowly, deliberately he drew back the hammer of his pistol, never removing me from his cold, dead stare.

Taking dead aim between his eyes, I pulled the trigger. There was a deafening barrel blast but nothing else. I missed. Bracken just sat on the bed and stared, barely even blinking his eyes.

Again I pulled the trigger, but to the same terrifying result. Nothing happened but a loud deafening noise.

Again I pulled the trigger, but this time it produced nothing but the click of an empty chamber.

"Thank you, Mister McKall. Your bravery and courage have made my job frightfully easy. The gun powder burns produced on your hands by those blanks should prove once and for all that you fired the fatal shots here tonight. What a tragedy. A murder/suicide at your hand. Bravo," he said. The blankness of his face was replaced, for just a moment, by a slight little smile.

Desperately, I pulled the trigger several more times. Click, Click, Click. Helplessly, I dropped the gun and looked back up at Bracken who was now holding his gun on me.

I looked at Valerie, whose eyes were gripped with the most intense mixture of fear and confusion I had ever seen.

"I'm sorry, Valerie. I am so...sorry," I said, not knowing what else to do or say.

It was of no comfort to her, simply adding to her confusion.

My arms straining under the weight of the door panel dropped and the panel clanked against the floor.

"Now Mister McKall, if you will turn around while I finish Miss Turpin," he said.

Meekly I dropped my head and turned around while slowly pulling the door panel into my hands.

Cautiously, I looked over my shoulder. Bracken was straddling Valerie with a knee on either side of her, sitting on her legs, pulling on her shirt in an effort to rip it off.

Suddenly with all my strength, I turned on him, swinging the door panel right at his face. Instinctively he raised his arms to shield his face, but the force of the blow knocked him from the bed onto the floor, his gun falling from his hand and sliding under a chest of drawers. Following the momentum of my swing, I landed on top of him.

Quickly I pulled myself up so that I was sitting on his chest, but before I could really gather myself, I felt his hands around my throat squeezing. The door panel prevented me from simply knocking his hands away. I grabbed his arms and tried to pry them away from my throat.

His arms were lean and I could feel his muscles ripple as he applied his grip tighter and tighter. I could not budge his hands nor could I draw any part of a breath. My only recourse was to get off of him and let him up.

I dove for the chest of drawers. I could see his gun on the floor in the very back corner. I reached under but the handcuffs and door panel prevented me from getting my hands very far under the chest. Getting to my knees in order to move the chest, I was jerked from behind by my shirt collar to the floor. A split second later the chest of drawers also landed on top of me.

I could not see Bracken, but in desperation I pushed back against the chest, throwing it in the same direction it had come from. Using my feet against the chest, I managed to pin Bracken against the wall. Again the gun slipped from his hands and slid across the floor into the hallway. I attempted to catch the gun as it slid by, and released just enough pressure on the chest that Bracken could push the chest away and dive for the gun.

As the chest crashed to the floor, I managed to regain enough of my balance to tackle Bracken mid-dive, landing on his back. Again and again, I pounded my hand down on his head, as he crawled for the gun. His strength amazed me. Nothing I could do seemed to stop his slow steady crawl for the gun. Giving up on sheer brute strength, I brought my cuffed hands over his head and around his neck. As I did the door panel opened up a large gash on his forehead. With all my remaining strength I pulled the handcuff chain as tight as I could around his throat. Still, he inched ever closer to the gun. I began driving my knee into his kidney again and again. Each blow brought a grunt of pain but did not slow his progress toward the gun.

The tighter and harder I pulled against his throat, the harder and more determined he struggled toward the gun.

After what seemed like several minutes he reached the gun. His fingers and hand shook violently as he reached out. Again, with all my weight I drove my knee into his kidney. His hand momentarily stopped. Planting my feet on the floor, I pulled back against his neck, dragging him away from the gun. But his hand grabbed the doorjamb, making it impossible to pull him further away.

I strained, not able to put all my strength into pulling him away. In a moment or two I began to lose the battle as he began again to inch closer and closer to the gun. His capacity for going without breath amazed me almost as much as his strength.

His hand reached the gun. I relinquished my grip on his throat and lunged over his head. Getting there a fraction of a second too late, I landed chest first on the panel. Bracken's hand was in place around the butt of the gun, his finger on the trigger. My hands, which were now pinned under the door panel floor, held the barrel. Before I realized my situation, Bracken fired the gun. The bullet ripped through the fleshy part of my palm. As the gun fired he snatched it from my grip. My legs and hips were still on his head, and he was gasping for his first breaths in what had to be over a minute.

My hand felt as though it were on fire and stabbing pain was shooting up my arm. Twisting and turning his arm and hands, he tried to get the gun and his arm from under me. Handcuffed and anchored by the door panel, I could not get either my good or my bad hand anywhere close to the gun. The barrel, hot from having been fired only seconds before, was burning my chest. Although I could not get the leverage needed for a hard blow, I used my knees to kick Bracken in the back of the head. Each time I delivered a blow, his forehead bounced hard off the wood floor.

Without warning, I rolled from my stomach to my back. This surprised Bracken, who had almost simultaneously decided to give one last yank of the gun. Without the expected resistance, he nearly fell backwards. As he righted himself I cocked my knee up by my chest and kicked him under his chin. Instantly he dropped unconscious to the floor. His legs folded awkwardly under him. The gun fell to the floor.

The blood from my hand was everywhere, and gave the appearance that I was more hurt than I really was. I was completely spent and lay on the floor for a second or two catching my breath before I thought again of Valerie. She was on the bed, tears streaming down her checks with her eyes shut as tightly as she could possibly hold them.

"It's alright, Valerie," I said as I began to get to my feet. "Everything is alright."

Cautiously she opened her eyes and looked around the room. I walked over, picked up Bracken's gun, and shoved it into my belt then began removing the gag from her mouth. There was still a lot of confusion in her eyes.

"I'm sorry you got caught up in all of this," I said as the gag fell from her mouth.

"You?...I don't..." she said through tears of relief and gasping breaths.

"It is over, try to relax," I said. The blood from my hand continued to spread.

"Are you all right?" she asked.

"He just got me in the hand," I said and held up my hand so that she could see the gunshot wound.

"Hold still and I'll try to untie your hands."

I WAS STILL untying her hands when Lt. James and a group of five uniformed police officers busted into the house and found us in the basement. Bracken was still unconscious on the floor.

James was the first into the room with his gun pulled.

"Are you alright, Ms. Turpin?" he asked and made a big show of removing the gun from my belt.

"I'm fine. I guess," she said, clearly confused by everything that had happened.

"Get Mister McKall some medical attention," James said to a female officer standing at the room's door. "And place him under arrest."

For a second Valerie sat motionless. The confusion on her face was clear. She started to say something, I'm not sure what. I don't know what Lt. James would have done had she been able to offer me a defense. But who could blame her for being confused and not really knowing for sure what had just happened.

"We'll sort it all out at the police station, Ms. Turpin. Don't worry," he said and then motioned to the officer to take me out of the room. I thought about offering some resistance but emotionally and physically I was too exhausted to do anything but comply.

An ambulance pulled up to Valerie's house just as the officer was escorting me out. The paramedic dressed my hand with a temporary bandage and insisted that I go to the hospital. I refused in favor of going to the police station and getting this whole thing sorted out once and for all.

TWENTY-TWO

TO THIS DAY, I don't know whether or not Lt. James was just following procedure or taking out some unexplained vendetta on me, but my temporary arrest dominated the evening news. I, of course, did not see any of it because I was at the Wasatch City Police Department trying to explain the complicated and admittedly unbelievable chain of events that had brought me handcuffed to Valerie Turpin's bedroom.

At one point I was left in a holding cell while Lt. James and his cadre interviewed Smitty at University Hospital. It took the better part of the next eight hours and a clear-headed Valerie to convince Lt. James he had arrested the wrong man and that the real culprit, one of them at least, was H. Robert Bracken.

The next day was a blur of media coverage and fast-moving events. Wasatch City PD spent the day retracting and explaining. The Consortium placed Tom Griggs on a leave of absence. The Governor issued a statement praising my bravery and calling for an FBI investigation. The FBI quickly complied.

I spent the morning at the hospital getting my hand treated and watching on TV as Lt. James answered questions put to him by the media. He had made them look foolish in the previous news cycle and it was now their turn to return the favor. Like hungry piranha, they picked his bones clean. I was too tired to really enjoy it, but I would be lying if I didn't say that it was quite satisfying seeing him answer for his arrogance.

Beckstead made a big production of visiting me in the hospital, mugging for the cameras and reporters stationed right outside the emergency room doors. Once in the room, he carried on for thirty minutes as if I was the hero he always thought I was. I thanked him for his support.

Finally at about 3:00 that afternoon I stepped out of the hospital and conducted an impromptu press conference of my own.

In the previous 24 hours I was cast as a power-hungry political hack responsible for at least three murders and gallant hero who, while being wrongly pursued by police, saved the life of a stalking victim and uncovered a conspiracy responsible for three murders. I hope you won't mind if we keep it as our little secret that neither story was entirely accurate.

OVER THE NEXT few weeks I had a few brief awkward meetings with Governor Beckstead, who denied that he had ever not believed me but obviously felt guilty about the way he handled the situation. He was relieved when a few weeks later I quietly and respectfully offered my resignation. My last day in the office provided a parade of staff members, who wanted to make sure that I knew that they had never doubted me—not for one second—and were sad to see me go. I joined in the charade and pretended that the trust between us had never been breached and wished them the best.

TWENTY-THREE

SMITTY'S ARTICLE, written nearly nine months after that awful night at Valerie's house is perhaps the best summation. It read:

Bracken Gets Half-Life in
Nuclear Deal
by Wayne Smith

Wasatch City—The final chapter in the Pishute Indians' ill-fated nuclear waste facility project was written today, when H. Robert Bracken was sentenced to a maximum sentence of 25 years for two counts of attempted first-degree murder and one count of kidnapping.

The sentencing concluded a nine-month long investigation by the Federal Bureau of Investigations.

Bracken first came under official suspicion when Wasatch City police answered a call of a domestic disturbance at the home of Wasatch City resident Valerie Turpin.

Upon arriving at the scene police found Turpin tied to her bed, Bracken unconscious on the floor and Sam McKall, a work colleague of Turpin's, handcuffed with a gunshot wound in the palm of his right hand.

Bracken, the great-grandson of Utah railroad magnate Theodore H. Bracken, had been stalking and terrorizing Turpin in order to conceal the theft of sensitive materials from her office pertaining to the proposed nuclear waste dump on the Pishute Indian Reservation in Utah's West Desert.

Bracken had been the owner of an 844-acre tract of land needed by the Consortium of utilities known as Waste Solutions, Inc. and stood to make tens of millions on the proposed project.

Shortly after the incident at the Turpin residence, at the request of the Bureau of Indian Affairs and local authorities, the FBI opened its own investigation into the incident and suspicious circumstances around the death of Pishute Tribal Council member Mary Leapingdeer, her son Jeff Leapingdeer, and State Senator Ralf Voss.

The thrust of the investigation centered on Bracken and Thomas Griggs, the project manager working for Waste Solutions, Inc.

Prosecutors refused to elaborate on whether Griggs may have had a role in the crimes, but named him in the 28-count indictment of Bracken as an "unindicted co-conspirator."

A third man, once thought to be a target of the FBI's investigation, Pishute Tribal Chief Jack Longnight, was exonerated several months into the investigation by the Justice Department, who offered Longnight an emphatically worded letter removing him from suspicion for any wrongdoing.

The indictments touched off a heated legal battle maneuvering between the Justice Department and Bracken's attorney, who offered what one Justice Department official called, "a tenacious and unrelenting" defense of their client.

The legal wrangling abruptly ended six weeks ago when both sides announced a plea bargain.

The deal, under which most of the state's political establishment chaffed, required Bracken to plead guilty to the attempted murders and one count of stalking and accept the maximum sentences for each crime. In exchange for Bracken's guilty plea, the rest of the charges, including the two counts of first-degree murder, were dropped, saving Bracken from the specter of a possible death sentence.

"We understand the dissatisfaction in some quarters with this outcome. In many ways, it is not very satisfying to me either," said Justice Department Attorney Jorge Perez. "But in the final analysis this deal offered the best chance that Mr. Bracken would spend a significant amount of time in prison for the crimes he committed."

Although prosecutors never offered a complete theory of the crime, attorneys close to the investigation have provided the following scenario:

Approximately 18 months ago the Consortium completed a deal with two major landowners in Utah's West Desert. The principal landowner was the Pishute Indian Tribe through its chief, Jack Longnight, and the owner of an 844-acre in-holding, Bracken. The deal, which was worth hundreds of millions to each party, was totally dependent on the successful siting of a nuclear waste facility on the leased land.

The first hurdle the project had to get over was the approval of the seven-member Tribal Council, which it did on a 4-3 vote after heavy arm-twisting by Jack Longnight.

One of those voting in favor of the project was Mary Leapingdeer, who was well known for her emphasis on traditional tribal values and as a tireless advocate for economic development on the reservation.

Immediately after her vote in favor of the project, Mary came under an intense lobbying effort by her son Jeff Leapingdeer, a San Francisco environmental attorney, to change her position.

No one can know for sure what transpired between mother and son, but it appears that Jeff was successful in persuading his mother to change her support to opposition. This shift is explained by Mary in a letter, obtained by the *Capitol Times* to a second son, Calvin Leapingdeer. (A picture of the letter accompanied the story.)

Here the chain of events becomes crucial. On the evening of August 3 Longnight stopped by Mary's home for a meeting which she had requested. At that meeting, according to Longnight, Mary told the chief about her change of heart and her plans to bring the project up for reconsideration at the Tribal Council meeting the following week.

Upon leaving the meeting, Longnight immediately phoned Griggs and told him about the problem. Phone records subpoenaed by the Justice Department show that Griggs immediately thereafter called Bracken at his Park Avenue, New York apartment. Bracken was on the next flight to Wasatch City. Twenty-four hours after his arrival, Mary Leapingdeer suffered a fatal fall in her shower. At first considered an accident, that fatality is now considered by investigators to have been the first of three murders perpetrated by Bracken.

Jeff Leapingdeer became suspicious of his mother's death and contacted the Tribal Police regarding his concerns. Their investigation uncovered no evidence of foul play.

Not satisfied, Jeff tried to contact the *Capitol Times* regarding his concerns. He died before his calls were returned in what San Francisco police still believe was an alcohol-related one-car accident. Subsequent FBI investigations have suggested that Jeff may have been lured to a meeting at the end of winding mountain road and while at the meeting, motor oil may have been added to the master brake cylinder of his car which caused the brakes to suddenly and completely lock up as he descended the mountain road, sending him to his death.

Here again the FBI was only able to uncover circumstantial evidence of Bracken's involvement, including hotel and airplane receipts.

Shortly after, the utility Consortium and the Tribe had announced the pending deal in the spring of last year. The late State Senator Ralf Voss uncovered some information, which he forwarded to Valerie Turpin, an attorney in the State Office of Legislative Research and General Council office, with a note that he would talk to her about the information upon his return to Wasatch City.

Per his request Turpin filed the document away and awaited the Senator's further instructions.

None were forthcoming. Voss was killed in a skiing accident which was never investigated by any law enforcement authority until the FBI began its investigation, some two months after the fact.

It is not clear how Bracken became aware of the documents, but shortly thereafter he began stalking Turpin, pretending to be obsessed with her, eventually breaking into her office and stealing the documents under the guise of vandalizing her office with perverted sexually explicit messages.

It was not known that the documents were missing until Sam McKall, then chief of staff to Governor LaGrand Beckstead, had learned of their existence and asked to see them.

Apparently this, or a similar turn of events, had been anticipated by Bracken, who began immediately to misconstrue the evidence of his stalking of Valerie Turpin to look as though it was being perpetrated by McKall. Bracken even followed McKall on a trip to Maine and made threatening phone calls to Turpin from a restaurant at which McKall was having dinner.

On another occasion, Bracken followed McKall to San Francisco and mugged one of the late Jeff Leapingdeer's co-workers, stealing her electronic office keys and using them to break into Jeff's office.

So convincing was Bracken's deception that Lt. Fred James, Wasatch City PD's lead investigator into Turpin's stalking, had zeroed in on McKall as the perpetrator, going so far as to arrest him for the crime only moments after McKall had saved Turpin and himself from being murdered by Bracken.

Faced with the irrefutable evidence of both Bracken's guilt and McKall's innocence, the Wasatch City Police Department released McKall and turned the investigation over to the FBI.

What little chance of success the nuclear

> waste dump had after the murderous conspiracy was uncovered, quickly vanished when the Justice Department listed Griggs as an unindicted co-conspirator.
>
> The five utility companies behind the proposed project have vehemently and repeatedly denied any knowledge of the crimes. This assertion seems to be supported by the FBI, which after an initial investigation dropped the companies and their officers, with the notable exception of Griggs, from their target list.
>
> In the end the investigation answered some important questions, left many more unanswered and could only manage to bring shaky and uneasy closure to three unjustified murders.

AS USUAL, Smitty had nailed the story. I don't know whether it is one of life's great ironies or simply a case of poetic justice, but as things turned out it was Smitty that did the job I had been hired to do—save the Beckstead Administration. Had Smitty not gotten curious about the message Jeff Leapingdeer left on his voice mail, the murders would have likely gone undetected and who knows if we would have been successful in stopping the Consortium. But as the dump proposal came crashing down, Beckstead's numbers began a steady rise, peaking in the days immediately after Smitty's story appeared in the *Capitol Times*.

Beckstead, of course, would never acknowledge Smitty's hand in saving his political hide. And to

Smitty it was the bitterest of pills. I enjoyed reminding them both of it on every possible occasion.

FINALLY, IT WAS summer again and the thing I liked most about Smitty's story was that I was reading it in a hammock overlooking York Beach, Maine.